"Sam, we've already said goodbye to each other...

"Why make this harder than it has to be?"

Sam laid his hands on Mia's shoulders and the heat of her body rose up to slide into his. "Hello isn't hard, Mia. Unless you're doing it right."

"Sam..."

He bent his head to hers and stopped when his mouth was just a breath away from her lips. Waiting for acceptance. For her to let him know that she shared what he was thinking, feeling.

"This could be a big mistake," she said, with a slow shake of her head.

"Probably," he agreed, knowing it wouldn't change anything.

Seconds passed and still he waited.

Finally, though, she dropped her purse to the floor, reached up to cup his face between her palms and said, "What's one more mistake?"

Dear Reader,

Oh, I love a Christmas book! During the holiday season, there are so many wonderful things happening that a romance set during that time has a special feeling to it.

In *Temptation at Christmas*, you'll experience a Christmas-themed cruise with Sam Buchanan and Mia Harper. Their divorce should be almost final—but turns out, the papers were never filed. So they're not as "ex" as they think.

Sam owns Fantasy Cruise lines, so Mia takes the cruise to tell Sam the news in person—and her family comes along as backup. What could go wrong?

They have fourteen days at sea to either find a way to save the marriage or to accept that what they'd once had is gone forever. Of course, shipboard romances are legendary, and these two have a head start.

So, when the shopping and wrapping are done, make yourself a cup of tea, curl up and dive into a Christmas romance. I really hope you enjoy this book, and the Christmas magic, as much as I did while writing it.

Happy reading!

Until next time,

Maureen

MAUREEN CHILD

TEMPTATION AT CHRISTMAS

HARLEQUIN
Desire

HARLEQUIN®
DESIRE™

Recycling programs
for this product may
not exist in your area.

ISBN-13: 978-1-335-20939-9

Temptation at Christmas

Copyright © 2020 by Maureen Child

This edition published by arrangement with Harlequin Books S.A.

For questions and comments about the quality of this book, please contact us at CustomerService@Harlequin.com.

Harlequin Enterprises ULC
22 Adelaide St. West, 40th Floor
Toronto, Ontario M5H 4E3, Canada
www.Harlequin.com

Printed in U.S.A.

Maureen Child writes for the Harlequin Desire line and can't imagine a better job. A seven-time finalist for the prestigious Romance Writers of America RITA® Award, Maureen is the author of more than one hundred romance novels. Her books regularly appear on bestseller lists and have won several awards, including a Prism Award, a National Readers' Choice Award, a Colorado Romance Writers Award of Excellence and a Golden Quill Award. She is a native Californian but has recently moved to the mountains of Utah.

Books by Maureen Child

Harlequin Desire

Rich Rancher's Redemption
Billionaire's Bargain
Tempt Me in Vegas
Bombshell for the Boss
Red Hot Rancher
Jet Set Confessions
The Price of Passion
Temptation at Christmas

Visit her Author Profile page at Harlequin.com, or maureenchild.com, for more titles.

You can also find Maureen Child on Facebook, along with other Harlequin Desire authors, at Facebook.com/harlequindesireauthors!

To Patti Hambleton,
because since we first met at six years old,
she has been the friend I could always count on.
The sister of my heart. And the one person
I never have to explain the jokes to!
I love you.

One

Sam Buchanan hated Christmas.

Always had, but this year, he had more reason than ever to wish he could wipe the "holiday season" off the calendar for good.

"So go on a Christmas cruise," he muttered darkly. "Good call."

He'd known it would be hard, but he wasn't one to step back from duty just because it was difficult. Sam had a business to take care of and he wouldn't let the personal get in the way of that.

Didn't mean he had to like it, though.

From the owner's suite at the top of the Fantasy Cruise Line ship, *Fantasy Nights*, Sam looked out on the curved bow with its sky-blue deck and the sea beyond…because he didn't want to look at the dock. San Pedro, California, harbor was crowded with passengers excited to get their cruise to Hawaii going and damned if he'd look down on a bunch of happy, celebrating people. Once the cruise got underway, he could hole up here, in his suite, only venturing out to check on his employees.

Sam took four cruises a year—on different ships in the Buchanan line—to maintain good communication with both crew and passengers. He'd always believed experiencing the cruises in person was the best way to keep his fingers on the pulse of what his guests and employees needed. Not to mention it was the only certain way to make sure those employees were doing their jobs to his expectations.

Gripping his coffee cup, he narrowed his gaze on the expanse of ocean waiting just beyond the harbor. Once they were on the open sea, he'd slip out of his suite, check in with the ship's captain and then do a walk through the restaurants.

He wasn't looking forward to it.

Normally, the Fantasy Cruise Line didn't allow children onboard. Adult-only cruises were their mainstay. But at Christmas, the rules were relaxed so that families could enjoy sailing together on their smaller, more intimate ships.

So for this cruise, not only would he be faced with miles of Christmas garland, brightly lit trees and piped-in Christmas carols, but there would be dozens of kids, hyped up on Santa and candy, to deal with as well. And still, he told himself, it was better to be on this cruise than in his own home where the *lack* of Christmas would taunt him even more completely.

"Yeah," he assured himself solemnly, "no way to win this year."

The phone on the wet bar rang and Sam walked to it. "Yes?"

"Captain says we sail in an hour, Mr. Buchanan."

"Fine. Thanks." He hung up and listened to the silence in the owner's suite. There would be plenty of it for the next couple of weeks and he was looking forward to it even as he dreaded it.

A year ago, things had been different. He'd met a woman on another cruise and two months later, they'd had a Christmas-themed wedding. And they had taken this Christmas cruise for their honeymoon. Yes, for Mia's sake, Sam had even given Christmas a shot. He hadn't thrown himself into it or anything, but he also hadn't been quite the Scrooge he usually was.

Now the marriage was gone. She was gone. And Christmas was back, just to rub it in.

He set his coffee cup down on the bar top, shoved both hands into the pockets of his black slacks and stared around the beautifully appointed room. The owner's suite was twelve hundred square feet of luxury. Teak floors gleamed in the sunlight, paintings of the sea and several of Sam's cruise ships lined the walls. On the ocean side of the suite, the wall was one-way glass, affording an incomparable view of the ocean and the wide balcony that stretched the length of the suite.

Leather club chairs and sofas were gathered atop a rich, burgundy throw rug in the middle of the living room and there were tables with lamps bolted onto them, in case of rough seas. There was a flat-screen television on the wall and a dining room off to one side.

There were two bedrooms and three bathrooms along with the private balcony/terrace that added an extra two hundred square feet to the suite. The master bedroom and en suite bath boasted a view of the sea from behind one-way glass. He could see out, but no one could see in.

And in spite of his surroundings, Sam felt...on edge. He stalked out to the terrace and let the cold wind slap at him. Glancing down at the nearly empty deck of the bow, Sam noticed a woman with long, wavy red hair and it felt as though someone had punched him in the chest.

"It's not her. Why the hell would she be on this cruise?"

Still, he couldn't look away. She wore white slacks and a long-sleeved green shirt and her hair lifted and twisted in the wind. Then she turned sideways and Sam saw that she was very pregnant. Disappointment tangled with relief inside him, until the redhead stopped, looked up and seemed to stab his stare with her own.

Mia?

His heart jolted and his hands fisted on the cold, white iron railing. She's *pregnant*? Why wouldn't she tell him? Why didn't she say *something*? What the hell was she doing here? And why didn't she take off her sunglasses so he could see the green eyes that had been haunting him for months?

But she didn't comply with that wish. Instead, she shook her head, clearly in disgust, and then stalked away, disappearing from view in less than a moment.

Mia. Pregnant.

Here.

Sam went inside, rushed across the room and hit the front door at a dead run. Somebody had better tell him something fast. He didn't waste time with a phone call. Instead he went down to the main deck where passengers were still filing onboard. The purser was there, along with two of the entertainment crew, to welcome people onto *Fantasy Nights*. Ordinarily, Sam would have been impressed with how easily his employees handled the streaming crowds—all smiles and conversations. But today, he needed answers.

"Mr. Wilson," Sam said and the purser turned. Instantly, the older man straightened up as if going to attention.

"Mr. Buchanan," he said with a nod. "Is there something I can help you with?"

"Yeah. Has a woman named Mia—" he almost said *Buchanan*, but Sam remembered at the last min-

ute that his ex-wife had returned to her maiden name
after the divorce "—Harper, checked in?"

The man quickly checked through the list of
names on the clipboard he held. Then he glanced
at his boss and said, "Yes sir. She did. A half hour
ago. She—"

That was Mia. A very pregnant Mia.

"Which suite is she in?"

He knew she had a suite because all of the staterooms on the *Fantasy Nights* were suites. Some more
luxuriously appointed than others but every suite on
this ship was roomy and inviting.

"It's the Poseidon, sir. Two decks down on the
port side and—"

"Thanks. That's all I need." Sam threaded his way
through the crowd already spilling into the atrium,
the main welcome spot on any ship.

On *Fantasy Nights*, the atrium was two stories of
glass-and-wood spiraling staircases, now draped in
pine garland. There was a giant Christmas tree in
the middle of the room boasting what looked to Sam
like a thousand twinkling, colored lights, along with
ornaments—that the passengers could also purchase
in the gift shop. There was a group of carolers in one
corner, and miles of more pine garland draped like
bunting all around the room.

Hanging from the ceiling were hundreds of
strands of blinking white lights, to simulate snow-
fall and on one wall, there were tables set up, laden
with Christmas cookies and hot chocolate.

Sam barely noticed. He didn't have time to wait for the elevator. Instead, he headed for the closest staircase and took them two at a time. He knew every ship in his fleet like the back of his hand, so he didn't need to check the maps on the walls to know where he was headed.

The Poseidon suite was one of their larger ones and he wondered why Mia had bothered to book a two-bedroom suite. If she was pregnant, why the hell hadn't she come directly to him months ago? He had no answers to too many questions racing through his mind, so Sam pushed all of them aside, assuring himself he'd solve this mystery soon enough.

The excited chatter of conversations and bursts of laughter from children and their parents chased him down the first hallway on the port side. On most cruise ships, hallways dividing the staterooms were narrow and usually dark in spite of carefully placed lighting. Fantasy Cruise Line hallways were wider than usual and boasted overhead lighting and brass wall sconces alongside every stateroom.

Here, the floorboards were also teak and on each door was attached a plaque describing the name of the suite itself. For example, he thought as he stopped outside Mia's suite, her doorway held the image of Poseidon, riding a whale, holding his trident high, as if ready to attack an enemy. He wondered if that was an omen for what was to come.

He didn't have long to think about it. He knocked and a moment later, the door was yanked open. Long red hair. Sharp green eyes. Green shirt. White pants. Pregnant belly.

But not Mia.

Her twin, Maya.

Was he feeling relief? Disappointment? Both? Sam just stared at her. Damned if he could think of anything to say.

Maya didn't have that problem. She glared at him then and snapped, "Happy anniversary, you bastard."

Almost instantly, Mia appeared behind her twin. Rolling her eyes at her sister's drama, she said, "Maya. Stop."

Her sister stared at her for a second or two. "Seriously? You're going to defend him?"

"Defend me from what?" Sam asked.

"What?" Maya repeated, shifting a hard look to him before turning back to her twin. "Really? Even now you want me to play nice?"

"Really." Mia tugged on her sister's arm. "I love you. Go away."

"Fine," Maya said, throwing both hands into the air. She threw one last hard look at Sam. "But I'm not going far…"

"What the hell?" Sam muttered, keeping a wary eye on the woman as she walked away.

This was not the way Mia had wanted to handle this. But then, nothing about this trip was how she'd wanted it. She hadn't planned on bringing her entire family with her, for instance. But there was nothing she could do about that now, except maybe keep Maya away from Sam.

"Yeah, she's not your biggest fan," Mia admitted, then stepped into the hallway, forcing him to move back to make room. She pulled the door closed behind her, leaned against it and lifted her gaze to the man of her dreams.

Well, she amended mentally, the *former* man of her dreams.

He was tall. She'd always liked that. Actually, it had been one of the first things she'd noticed about him the night they met. She was five feet nine inches tall, so meeting a man who was six foot four had been great. That night she'd been wearing three-inch heels and she'd still had to look up to meet his eyes.

And they were great eyes. Pale, pale blue that could turn from icy to heat in a blink of time. His black hair was a little too long for the CEO of a huge company, but it was thick and shiny and she'd once loved threading her fingers through it. In fact, even after everything that had happened between them, Mia's fingers itched to do it again.

He was wearing a suit, of course. Sam didn't do "relaxed." He wore his elegantly tailored suits as if he'd been born to wear them. And maybe he had been, Mia mused. All she was sure of was that beneath that dark blue, pinstriped suit, was a body that looked as if it had been sculpted by angels on a very good day.

Her heartbeat jumped skittishly and she wasn't

surprised. She had met him and married him within a two-month, whirlwind span and though the marriage had lasted only nine months—technically—she knew it might take her years to get over Sam Buchanan.

Then he started talking.

"What are you doing here?"

Mia scowled. "Well, that's a very gracious welcome, Sam. Thank you. Good to see you, too."

He didn't look abashed, only irritated. "What's going on, Mia? Why is my ex-wife on this cruise?"

Hmm. More 'wife' than 'ex', she thought, but they'd get to that.

"This was the only way I could find to get you alone long enough to talk."

He snorted and pushed one hand through that great hair. "Really. You couldn't just pick up the phone?"

"Please." She waved that away. "Like I didn't try? Your assistant kept putting me off, telling me you were in a meeting or on the company jet heading off to Katmandu or something…"

"Katmandu?"

"Or somewhere else exotic, far away and out of reach apparently, of my phone."

Sam tucked his hands into his slacks pockets. "So you take a fifteen-day cruise?"

Mia shrugged. "Seemed like a good idea at the time."

"With Maya."

"And her family."

He glanced down the hallway and then to the closed door, as if expecting to see Joe and the kids pop out of hiding. "You're kidding."

"Why would I kid?"

The door flew open and Maya was there, glaring at him. Mia sighed, but gave up trying to rein in her twin.

"Why wouldn't she bring her family along as backup when she has to face you?" Maya asked.

"Backup?" He pulled his hands free, folded his arms across his chest and glared at the mirror image of Mia. "Why the hell would she need backup?"

"As if you didn't know," Maya snapped. "And another news flash for you, Mom and Dad are here too, and they're not real happy about it."

He looked at Mia. "Your parents are here?"

She lifted both hands helplessly. Mia hadn't actually *invited* any of her family along on this trip. She'd simply made the mistake of telling her twin what she was planning and Maya had taken it from there. Her family was circling the wagons to keep her from being hurt again. Hard to be angry with the people who loved you because they wanted to protect you.

Also hard to not be frustrated by them.

"Are Merry and her family here too?" Sam asked. "Cousins? Best friends?"

"Merry didn't trust herself to see you," Maya snapped.

Thank God, their older sister Merry had decided

to stay home with her family or things would have been even wilder. It was comforting to realize that at least one member of her family was sane.

"Maya," Mia said on a sigh, "you're not helping. Close the door."

"Fine but I'll be listening anyway," she warned and slammed the door so that the sound echoed along the hallway.

And she would be, too, Mia knew. "Merry stayed home to keep the bakery running," she said. "Christmas is our busiest time of the year."

"Yeah, I remember."

"So busy," she continued as if he hadn't spoken, "Mom and Dad are cruising to Hawaii, but they're going to fly home from there to help Merry."

"I don't get it."

"Which part?"

"All of it." He shook his head, took her arm and steered her further from the door, no doubt because he knew that Maya was indeed listening to everything they said. "I still don't know why you're here. Why you felt like you needed an army just to face me."

"Not an army. Just people who love me." Mia pulled her arm free of his grasp because the heat building up from his touch was way too distracting. How was she supposed to keep her mind on why she was there when he was capable of dissolving her brain so easily?

And that, she told herself, was exactly why the family had come along.

"We have to talk."

"Yeah, I guessed that much," he said, shooting a glance at the still closed door.

Just being this close to Sam was awakening everything inside her and Mia knew that she was really going to need her family as a buffer. Because her natural impulse was to move in closer, hook her arms around his neck and pull his head to hers for one of the kisses she had spent the last few months hungering for—and trying to forget.

But that wouldn't solve anything. They would still be two people connected only by a piece of paper. They had never been married in the same way her parents were. The Harpers were a unit. A team, in the best sense of the word.

While Mia and Sam had shared a bed but not much else. He was always working and when he wasn't, he was locked in his study, going over paperwork for the business or making calls or jetting off to meetings with clients and boat builders and— anyone who wasn't *her*.

Passion still simmered between them, but she'd learned the hard way that desire wasn't enough to build a life on. She needed a husband who was there to talk to, to laugh with—and they hadn't done that nearly enough. She wanted a man who could bend and not be constricted by his own inner rules and Sam didn't know how to bend. How to compromise.

Mia had tried. Had fought for their marriage but when she realized that only she was trying, she gave up.

If he'd been willing to work on things with her, they'd still be together.

"Fine then. We'll talk," Sam said, still keeping a wary eye on the door of her suite as if expecting Maya to leap out again.

Mia would not have been surprised. Her twin was very protective.

"But not here where Maya's listening to everything we say..." He frowned thoughtfully. "Once we're underway, I need to meet with some of the crew, check on a few things..."

She sighed. "Of course you do."

One eyebrow lifted. "You know I take these cruises to get the information I need on how our ships are operating."

"I remember." In fact, she recalled the cruises they'd taken together after they were married. Two of them. One to the Bahamas. One to Panama. And on each of them, the only time she really saw her new husband was at night, in their bed. Otherwise, Sam the Workaholic was so busy, it had been as if she were traveling alone.

"That's why we're here. On this ship," Mia said. "I knew you'd be taking this cruise."

He laughed. "Even knowing I hate the Christmas cruises?"

"Yes. Because it helps you avoid having to be at home with a non-Christmas," she said.

His frown went a little deeper. Apparently, he didn't like the fact that she could read him so easily. But it hadn't been difficult. Sam hated Christmas and no matter how Mia had tried to drag him, kicking and screaming into the spirit of the holiday, he would not be moved. Her family had planned their wedding and he'd been surrounded by holly leaves, poinsettias and pine garlands. After the wedding, he'd given in to her need to have a tree and lights and garland, but he'd admitted to her that if she weren't there, Christmas would have been just another day at his house.

She'd thought then and still believed that it was just sad. In her family, Christmas season started the day after Thanksgiving. Lights went up, carols were played, gifts were bought and wrapped and her sisters' kids wrote and then revised letters to Santa at least once a week.

She'd tried to get him to tell her why he hated that holiday so much, but not surprisingly, he wouldn't talk about it. How could she reach a man if every time she tried to breach his walls, he built them higher?

So yes, she'd known that Sam would take a Christmas cruise to avoid being at home in what was probably a naked house, devoid of any holiday cheer. It hadn't made much sense to her until she realized that Christmas decorations meant nothing to him, but a house devoid of those very decorations only made him remember that he was different than most people. That he'd chosen to live in a gray world when others were celebrating.

"These cruises are booked months out," he said. "How did you manage to get suites for the whole family?"

"Mike arranged it."

Sam's eyes flashed and she wasn't surprised. His younger brother had always been on Mia's side and thought their separation was the worst thing to happen to Sam. So Mia had counted on his brother's help to "surprise" Sam on this cruise.

"Mike? My own brother?"

She might have enjoyed the complete shock stamped on Sam's features, if she wasn't worried that this situation could start an open war between the brothers.

"Don't fault him for it either," Mia warned. "He was helping me out, not betraying you,"

"What did you think I'd do to him?" he demanded and she heard the insult in his voice.

"Who knows?" She threw both hands up. "Fly to Florida and toss him in the ocean? Keelhaul him? Throw him in a dungeon somewhere? Chain him to a wall?"

His eyes went wide and he choked out a laugh. "I live in a penthouse condo, remember? Sadly, it doesn't come equipped with a dungeon."

Oh, she remembered the condo. Spectacular

with an amazing view of the ocean through a wall of glass. And she remembered spending too much time alone in that luxurious, spacious place, because her husband had chosen to bury himself at work.

Okay, that worked to stiffen her spine.

"Fine," she said. "Then we're agreed. You don't give Mike grief."

"Or a Christmas bonus," he muttered.

"He's your partner, not your employee." Shaking her head, Mia snapped, "You're going to give him a hard time anyway, aren't you?"

"I was kidding."

"Were you?" she asked.

"Mostly. You know what? Forget about Mike." Sam looked her square in the eye and asked, "Why are you here, Mia? And why'd you bring your family with you?"

She had needed the support because frankly, she didn't trust herself around Sam. One look at him and her body overrode her mind. She had to be strong and wasn't sure she could do it on her own. Still, she wasn't going to tell him that.

"They wanted to take a cruise and I needed to be here to talk to you, so we all went together."

"Sure. Happy coincidence. And why did you need to see me?"

"That's going to be a longer conversation."

"Does it include why you picked our anniversary to ambush me on a cruise ship?"

She could have kicked her twin. Maya wishing him a *Happy Anniversary* had been exactly the wrong thing to say. Mia loved that her family was so protective of her—and so really furious with Sam. But this was her life and she'd handle it her way. And reminding Sam about their anniversary, as if she were upset about it, wasn't her way. Of course, she *was* shaken by the fact that she was here to talk divorce with her husband on their first anniversary, but that didn't matter really, did it? Their marriage had ended months ago. What was happening now was just a formality.

And if he'd forgotten their anniversary, then Maya had just reminded him and that was infuriating, too. How could he forget? Was their all-too-brief marriage really that un-memorable? Was she? God knew, she'd forgotten *nothing* about her time with Sam.

Heck, just remembering the nights spent in his arms made her heart beat faster and her blood heat up until she felt like she had a fever. It was so hard to be this close to him and not lean in to kiss him. Touch his cheek. Smooth his hair back from his forehead. She muffled a sigh.

And all of this would have been much easier to handle if he didn't look so good.

From the first moment they'd met, on one of his cruise ships, Mia had been drawn to him. It had felt then like an electrical attraction and it seemed that nothing had changed there. His pale blue eyes still looked at her as if she were the only woman in the world. His mouth still made her want to nibble at his bottom lip. And she knew firsthand what it was like to have those strong, muscular arms wrapped around her and oh boy, she'd love to feel that again—even knowing it would be a huge mistake.

She could be in serious trouble.

"Are you okay?"

His question snapped her brain out of a really lovely fantasy and for that she was grateful. Sort of.

"Yeah, I'm fine." She looked up and down the corridor before turning her gaze back to his. "I didn't choose to find you on our anniversary. It just worked out that way. And like I said, we need to talk and I don't think this hallway is the place to do it."

"You're right." He glanced at the closed door behind which Maya was no doubt lurking. "But I'm not doing it with your sister around, either."

Mia laughed shortly. "No. Not a good plan. I'll come to you once I make sure Mom and Dad are settled in. And I want to help Maya with the kids…"

"Fine. Once we get into open water, give me an hour, then come to my suite."

She watched him walk away and her mouth went dry. Mia hated that her instinct was to chase him down and leap at him. She'd been doing so well, too. She was only dreaming about him three or four times a week now. Seeing him again, though, spending the next two weeks together on the same ship, was going to start up the fantasies and the desire all over again.

And there was zero way to avoid it.

Two

Mia being onboard this ship had already destroyed Sam's concentration. For an hour, he talked with the Captain, studied weather patterns with the First Officer charged with navigation, then finally had a meeting with the Chief Security Officer to get a report on any possible situations.

Through it all, he heard his employees but didn't listen with the same intensity he usually brought to his visits. How could he, when his mind kept drifting to his ex-wife?

Why did she have to look so damn good? And smell even better? He'd forgotten—or convinced himself—that he'd forgotten that subtle scent of summer that somehow clung to her. Her lotion?

Shampoo? He'd never really investigated it because it hadn't mattered to him *how* that scent appeared— he had simply enjoyed it.

And now it was with him again.

Haunting him again.

"And it's Michael's fault," he muttered. Standing on the private deck of his suite, Sam gripped his cell phone, ordered it to "Call Michael," then waited impatiently for his brother to pick up.

"Hey, Sam! How's it going?"

Scowling at the sailboats skimming the water in the distance, Sam blurted out, "You know exactly how it's going."

Michael laughed. "Ah…so you've seen Mia."

"Yes, I've seen her. And her twin. And apparently the rest of the family is aboard, too. What the hell were you thinking?" Sam curled one fist around the thick rail. The Plexiglas wall for safety only rose as high as the handrail. He wanted the feel of the wind against his face and right now, he was hoping it would cool him off. "I can't believe you did this. I'm your *brother*. Where's the loyalty?"

"Why wouldn't I do it?" Michael argued. "I like Mia. I like who you were when you were with her."

"What's that supposed to mean?"

His brother sighed. "It means that she was good for you. You laughed more back then."

"Yeah, everything was great until it wasn't."

That time with Mia hadn't lasted. As he'd known going into the marriage that it wouldn't. And even knowing that it would probably end badly, Sam had married her because he hadn't been able to imagine life without her. He'd risked failure and failed. Now, not only did he not have Mia, he had memories that continued to choke him during long, empty nights.

"We're divorced, Michael. It's over. You setting this up isn't helping any."

"It was helping Mia," his brother countered, then asked, "and if it's over, why is this bugging you so much?"

Good question.

"Look, I don't know why she had to see you, but when she asked, of course I did what I could."

Naturally, Michael would offer to help. That was just who he was. Some of the anger drained away as Sam realized how different he and his younger brother were. When their parents divorced, the kids were split up. Michael went to Florida with their mother while Sam stayed in California with their father.

They'd stayed close because they'd worked at it, even though they were only together whenever court-mandated visits to the non-custodial parent kicked in. Their father had been a hard man with strict rules for how Sam lived his life. Their mother was a kind-hearted woman who hadn't been able to live with that hard man.

So Sam grew up with the knowledge that marriage was a trap and never lasted—his father after all, had been married four times. As a father, he was disinterested, barely aware of Sam's existence. While Michael saw the other side of things with a mother who eventually remarried a man who had loved Michael as his own.

Now Sam was divorced and Michael was engaged and Sam sincerely hoped his little brother would have better luck in the marriage department than he himself had.

Mike was speaking, so Sam tuned in. "Why don't you just enjoy the situation?"

Sam was stunned speechless—but that didn't last. "*Enjoy* having my ex and her family—who all hate me, by the way—traveling with me for the next two weeks? Yeah, not gonna happen."

Michael laughed, damn it.

"Are you *scared* of the Harpers?"

"No."

Yes.

He hadn't known back then how to deal with a family who defended each other. Who listened. Who actually gave a damn. And he still didn't have a clue.

His brother knew him too well, that was the problem. Once they were grown the two of them had made time for each other. Building a relationship that might have been denied them because of the way they were raised. When their father died, and the business had come to the two of them, they'd carved out a workable solution that suited both men.

Michael took care of the east coast cruises, Sam had the west coast. They made major decisions for the company together and trusted each other to do what was best for the growth they both wanted to see happen.

"Okay, I admit that having her family there might be a little problematic."

"Yeah, you could say that."

"So fine. Ignore the family, enjoy Mia."

Oh, Sam would love to enjoy Mia. Every instinct he had was clamoring at him to go and find her. To pull her into his bed and never let her out again. But going there wasn't good for either of them. In their brief marriage it had become crystal clear that Sam and Mia weren't going to work out. She wanted more from him than he could give. Bottom line? They didn't belong together and they'd both acknowledged that in less than a year. Why stir the embers just to get burned again?

"For God's sake, Sam," Michael continued, "you haven't seen her in months."

He was aware.

"Yeah well, she'll be here soon to tell me why she's on this cruise in the first place."

And he couldn't wait to hear it. Had she planned to be here on their anniversary? Or was that just happenstance as she'd said? Did it matter? Either way their anniversary wasn't a celebration, but more a reminder of mistakes made.

He never should have married Mia, Sam knew that. But he'd done it anyway and so he'd only set Mia up for pain. That he hadn't intended, but it had, apparently, been unavoidable. Hell, maybe that was why she was here. Just to let him know that she was over him and moving on with her life.

Why tell him at all?

And even if she wanted him to know, why book a cruise for that?

Scowling at an ocean that didn't care what he was feeling or thinking, Sam heard Michael's voice as if from a distance.

"That's great. Talk to her about whatever it is she needs to tell you. And when you're done, keep talking."

"What am I supposed to say?"

"Wow. This is embarrassing. You're my big brother. And you can't figure out how to talk to a woman you were married to?" Michael took a breath and sighed it out. "Maybe you could tell her you miss her."

He straightened up. "What would be the point? She left me, remember?"

Sam remembered it well and didn't really want to revisit the memory.

"Yeah, I remember. Did you ever ask yourself why?"

"The reason doesn't matter. She left. I moved on. Done."

"Sure you did," Michael said. "Talk to her anyway. Maybe you'll surprise each other."

Sam snorted. "I don't like surprises."

"How are we related again?"

In spite of everything, Sam grinned and stared out at the ocean. "Beats the hell outta me."

"Me, too," Mike said, laughing. "Good luck on the cruise. I hope Mia drives you insane."

"Thanks."

"No problem—oh and Sam, Merry Christmas!"

"Not funny."

"Yeah it is," Mike said, still laughing as he hung up.

Then Sam was alone with the wind, the sea…and the faint sounds of Christmas carols drifting up from the lower deck. Just perfect.

The Buchanan cruise ships were much smaller than the mega ships most companies sailed these days.

Instead of thousands of people crowding a ship that offered sometimes very small cabins, there were only two hundred passengers total on a Buchanan ship and each cabin was a suite that didn't make one feel as if the walls were closing in.

But, Mia thought, it also meant that she felt the movement of the ocean more than she might on the bigger ships. Some people didn't care for that, but she loved it. She'd discovered her sea legs on the first cruise she'd taken—when she'd met Sam and her whole life had changed.

A year ago, she'd fallen in love and felt that the cruise was almost magical. Now, the magic was gone, but she was once again sailing on a cruise with the man she had believed was her future. She'd been foolish, believing that love at first sight was real and substantial and that the two of them together could do anything.

It hadn't taken long before Mia had realized that it *wasn't* the two of them. It was just her. Alone in a beautiful home with a man who seemed reluctant to do anything to save their marriage.

"Mrs. Buchanan."

Mia looked up to smile at one of the crew she knew from other cruises. About thirty, the man had blond-streaked brown hair, green eyes and wore the short-sleeved red polo shirt and white slacks that were the Fantasy Cruise Line uniform.

"Nice to have you aboard," he said.

"Thank you, Brandon," she answered, and didn't bother correcting him about the whole *Mrs. Buchanan* thing. Because honestly, until Sam signed those papers, she *was* Mrs. Buchanan, watching him as he hurried past intent on whatever he was doing.

Brandon walked away at top speed and she watched him go. She had to wonder how many of this crew she knew from her time with Sam. And she knew that even if Brandon was the *only* familiar face, by the time the cruise was over, she would know most of them.

Smaller ships meant a higher than usual crew to passenger ratio. At the end of the fourteen-day trip to Hawaii, the *Fantasy Nights* would feel like a small, insular village, where everyone knew everyone else.

"There's an upside and a downside to that though," she murmured and continued along the deck to the nearby staircase. Gossip would fly through the ship. And no doubt people would be talking about her and Sam, just as they had talked about them a year before on that first cruise.

Shaking her head, she ordered herself to stop thinking about Sam and try to enjoy being on the ship, seeing the ocean stretch out forever. Feeling the wind on her face and through her hair and listening to the distant shrieks and laughter of the kids onboard.

Christmas was stamped all over the sleek boat and she knew that had to be irritating to Sam. He didn't like the holiday at all and had only grudgingly accepted not only their Christmas themed wedding, but the Christmas tree she'd brought into their condo last year.

Since he was a kid, Christmas had been an exercise in emptiness. Sam's world was so wildly different from anyone else's that he never even tried to explain what it was about that holiday that left him feeling hollowed out. Who would understand?

Thinking back on it now, Mia wondered if the fact that he didn't like Christmas was part of the reason they just hadn't worked out. Well, maybe not the reason. But certainly a sign of things to come. She loved Christmas and everything it promised—hope, joy, love. And Sam tended toward the dark side.

Even as that thought registered, she shook her head.

It wasn't as if he was some evil mastermind or something—but he was more cynical than she was. More likely to see the downside than the up. Which was strange, since he was a masterful businessman and didn't you have to be optimistic to run a multimillion-dollar company?

She caught herself as she started going down the all too familiar path of trying to figure out Sam. It was an exercise in futility because the man simply didn't let anyone in long enough to actually *know* him.

"You've already spent months trying to figure Sam out, Mia," she lectured herself. "It's too late now, so just give it up already."

Taking a deep breath, Mia let go of the convoluted thoughts roiling through her mind and instead focused on where she was at the moment. Even though the reason for taking this cruise was a hard one, there was no reason she couldn't appreciate her surroundings.

There were brass pots displaying poinsettias bolted to the deck. Pine garlands were strung along the railings and the cushions on the chairs and lounges were a bright red and white. She smiled to herself as she realized that the whole ship felt like a Christmas snow globe, with the decorations and the happy people trapped inside the glass, just waiting for a giant hand to give it a shake.

The only way it could have been more perfect was if she didn't have to face her ex-husband and tell him they weren't as "ex" as they'd both believed. But she was only on this ship to confront Sam and get this whole thing settled, so the best thing she could do was to just get on with it.

Mia had plans, starting in January and she had to get this taken care of before she could move forward. She was tired of standing still. She wanted a future and the only way she was going to get it was to build it herself.

And still, as she made her way along the deck, Mia looked out at the sea, and paused briefly to watch the waves froth. She heard the slap of the water against the keel and took a deep breath of the cold, salty air. She smiled, in spite of the turmoil grumbling inside her.

Her family was upstairs in the atrium, no doubt huddled around the cookies and hot chocolate. She knew Maya's kids, Charlie and Chris, were already planning to explore the Snow Room that had been set up for children's play. Artificial snow, made just for the holiday cruise, was going to be very popular, especially with California kids who didn't get many chances to throw a snowball.

She kept walking, taking the stairs up, because it was faster than going inside and waiting for an elevator. Besides, she thought, as she looked out at the ocean, you didn't get a view from an elevator.

But no matter what she tried to tell herself about the view, the truth was, she was stalling. The thought of talking to Sam again had her unsettled. Off-balance.

He'd always made her feel that way, though. It looked to her like nothing had changed.

On the top deck, Mia walked toward the owner's suite. She knew exactly where it was, because that suite was positioned in exactly the same spot on every Buchanan ship. The closer she came to that wide, closed door though, the more her stomach jittered and the faster her heart raced.

"Damn it."

This should be easier. She'd cried Sam out of her system months ago. Their marriage was over. So why the hell could the very thought of him make her want to go all gooey?

"Because apparently, I have a masochistic streak," she muttered, then knocked before she could talk herself out of it.

When Sam opened the door, her gaze went straight to his. That cool, pale blue was fixed on her as if she were the only thing in the universe. Mia sighed. Sam was the one man who had ever looked at her like that. As if nothing else, in that moment, mattered. The only man who could make her knees weak with a glance. The only man who made her want to crawl into his bed and never leave it.

Which is exactly why you're in this mess, her mind whispered.

A year ago, she'd followed her heart—and her hormones—and had married the man of her dreams. Only to watch those dreams crumble into dust.

She kept that thought at the forefront of her mind as she said, "Hello, Sam."

Nodding sharply, Mia walked past him into the well-appointed suite. Her gaze swept the room in spite of the reason she was there. How could she not admire the space? The view of the sea, provided by the French doors and the wall of glass, was immense. It reminded her of the view from his condo at the beach, only here, she was much closer to that ocean, almost a part of it.

Breathtaking. And so was the rest of the room. Hardwood floors, jewel-toned rugs scattered across the honey-colored planks. A couple of sofas, that looked soft enough to sink into and easy chairs drawn together, facing the view that demanded attention.

"Well please," Sam muttered from behind her. "Come in."

She whirled around to face him, mindful of keeping a few feet of space between them. "Sam. We've got a problem."

"I don't think *we* have anything anymore."

He folded his arms over his broad, muscular chest and dipped his head down to stare at her. It was a technique he used. That professor-to-stupid-student glare. And as often as he might have used it on everyone else, that look had never worked on her before and it didn't now, either.

"You're wrong," she said shortly.

One eyebrow lifted.

She still didn't know how he did that.

"Okay," she said, "here it is. You know how *we* signed the divorce papers?"

"I recall," he said flatly.

"And *we* overnighted them in?"

"How about *we* get to the point?" His arms dropped to his sides. "What's this about, Mia?"

"Well, it seems we aren't as divorced as we thought we were."

Sam's brain short-circuited.

That was the only explanation for him being unable to think of a damn thing to say in response. Of course, it might have been being so close to Mia that was shutting his brain down, but that didn't make him feel any better about the situation.

The whole idea of what she was saying was preposterous. Ridiculous. He'd accepted his failure. Forced himself to acknowledge that he'd hurt the one woman in the world he valued. He'd lived through it, put it behind him.

Of course they were divorced.

But if they weren't…something that might have been hope rose up in him briefly, but Sam squashed it in an instant. No. Screw that, he wasn't going down that road. They were divorced. It was over.

"How is that possible?" He shook his head and held up one hand. "No. Never mind. It's not possible," he finally blurted.

"Apparently, it is." Mia tucked both hands into

the pockets of her white slacks, then pulled them free again.

Sam wasn't surprised. She'd always used her hands when she talked. And she did now.

Waving her left hand, he noticed the absence of her wedding rings and felt a twinge—of what, he didn't know. He wondered what she'd done with the gold, diamond-crusted band and the matching engagement ring he'd given her. Wasn't his business, of course, and simple curiosity would have to wait for another time. But it surprised him to note that it bothered him to see her not wearing the damn things.

Besides, he had to hear what she was saying rather than concentrating on her hands or the way that emerald-green silk shirt made her eyes an even richer, deeper green than usual. Her golden-red hair was long and loose laying across her shoulders, sliding against her neck and it was all Sam could do to keep from reaching out and touching her.

"So it turns out the overnight driver who was supposed to deliver our divorce papers to the court…"

"What?"

"He didn't." She shrugged helplessly. "He had a heart attack at work and when they went in to clean out his apartment, they found *mountains* of undelivered mail. The poor guy was a hoarder, I guess, and kept most of the packages he was supposed to deliver."

Sam couldn't believe this.

"Apparently, they even found forty-year-old

Cabbage Patch dolls!" She shook her head and sighed. "Poor little kids never got the dolls they wanted."

"Seriously?" he asked. "You're worried about kids who are now in their fifties or sixties?"

"Well, yes." She frowned at him and lifted both hands in a helpless shrug. "People are slowly being notified about this mess and I got word just last week."

"Last week?" She'd known they were still married for a week? "Why the hell didn't they notify me?"

"Probably because it was my name on the return address on the priority envelope."

Sam took a few long strides, taking him further away from the woman watching him so closely, then he turned around to face his *wife*. Not ex. Wife.

Scrubbing both hands across his face, he then let his hands fall to his sides. "So we're still married."

"I know what you're feeling. I couldn't believe it either. So now you see the problem."

He slowly walked toward her. "I see a problem, yeah. What I don't see is the big emergency that caused Michael to dump passengers off this cruise to make room for you and your family." Staring down into her eyes, he watched her closely as he asked, "Why the hell was it so important you get on this cruise to tell me something you could have handled back home with a damn phone call?"

She tipped her head back to look up at him. "This really isn't something I wanted to do over the phone and you were in Germany last week. This cruise was the first chance I had to talk to you in person."

"Okay. I get that." He hadn't exactly been easy to get a hold of lately. Since he and Mia had split up, Sam had kept even busier than he had been before and he wouldn't have thought that possible. Traveling, working, staying away from home as much as possible because the emptiness of his condo echoed with memories he'd rather not think about.

Mia kept her gaze on his as she dipped one hand into her black leather purse and drew out an envelope. Holding it out to him, she said, "My attorney drew up a new set of papers—same as the others. All you have to do is sign them and when we get home, I'll take them to the courthouse myself."

He looked at the envelope but didn't make a move to take it. They were still married. He didn't know how he felt about that. Michael had been right, Sam *had* missed Mia. More than he had expected. More than he wanted to admit. And now she was back. But nothing had changed. This delay in ending their marriage only meant the pain of failure would be drawn out.

"Why can't they just use the first set of papers?" he asked suddenly. "Why the need for new ones?"

"I don't know…" She waved her left hand again. "My lawyer thought it would be best this way and really? After I heard all about this, I didn't ask a lot of questions. I just want to get this done and over."

Looking into those forest-green eyes of hers, Sam

felt a punch of heat and regret slam into him. Didn't matter that she'd left him. He thought that he would probably *always* want her. For the last few months, he'd tried to push her out of his mind. He'd traveled the world and still the memory of her had chased him. And now she was here, standing in front of him and it was all he could do to keep from reaching for her. Hell, they were still married. They had a fourteen day cruise stretching out in front of them. Why shouldn't they spend that time together? Call it one last hurrah? She wanted divorce papers signed. So, maybe they could make a deal, he thought suddenly. That all depended on just how important this divorce was to her.

"You seem pretty eager," he said.

Her gaze narrowed on his. "Sam, we were done months ago. This is just the final step—one we thought we'd already taken. Why wouldn't I want it all finished?"

"No reason," he muttered, wondering if a deal was a bad idea. Of course it was a bad idea—but that didn't mean he wouldn't suggest it. He had to silently admit that it stung to see how impatient she was to cut him loose. He could remember a time when all they wanted was to be together. Hell, he still wanted that. And he could see from the heat in her eyes that she felt the same.

They were still married.

He was here, with his *wife*, and suddenly, divorce seemed light-years away. Moving in closer, he saw her take a deep breath and hold it and knew she was feeling the same pull he was. Her eyes were flashing, her lips parted as her breath came in short puffs.

"What're you doing?" Her voice came out in a strained whisper.

"I'm saying hello to my wife," he countered and gave her a half smile.

She slapped one hand to his chest. "The fact that we're still married is a technicality."

"Always liked technicalities."

Especially this one. Hell, even knowing their marriage was over didn't get rid of the desire pulsing inside him. The ache he'd carried around in the center of his chest was easing now because she was here. Because her scent had wrapped itself around him. And one look into her eyes told him she felt the same, though knowing Mia, she'd never admit to that.

"Sam, we've already said goodbye to each other," she reminded him. "Why make this harder than it has to be?"

He laid his hands on her shoulders and the heat of her body rose up to slide into his. "Hello isn't hard, Mia. Unless you're doing it right."

"Sam…"

He bent his head to hers and stopped when his mouth was just a breath away from her lips. Waiting for acceptance. For her to let him know that she shared what he was thinking, feeling.

"This could be a big mistake," she said, with a slow shake of her head.

"Probably," he agreed, knowing it wouldn't change anything.

Seconds passed and still he waited. Damned if he'd take what he wanted if she wasn't willing. Finally though, she dropped her purse to the floor, reached up to cup his face between her palms and said, "What's one more mistake?"

"That's the spirit."

He kissed her, pulling her up against him, wrapping his arms around her and holding her tightly.

Three

Sam's mouth covered hers, his tongue parted her lips and she opened for him eagerly, willingly. Then he was lost in the heat of her. Her taste, her scent, filled him and he wondered vaguely how he'd managed to breathe without her these last months.

Their tongues met in a tangle of desire that pulsed between them like a shared heartbeat. Her breath brushed against his cheek, her sigh sounded in the stillness and Sam lost himself in her. For this one moment, he was going to simply revel in having her back in his arms.

However briefly.

When he dropped his hand to that sweet butt of

hers though, she gasped and pulled back. Breathing deeply, she held up one hand and shook her head.

"Oh no you don't," she said. "A kiss hello is one thing, but we're not going to do what you think we're going to do."

"And what do I think?" he asked, grinning at her.

"The same thing I'm thinking," she said and when he took a step toward her again, she skipped backward. "Seriously, Sam, I'm not going to bed with you."

"Why not? We're married."

"For now," she said.

"I'm only talking about now." Sam moved in another step or two.

"That's the problem," she snapped. "Right there. You never thought about anything beyond the *now*."

Okay, that stopped him. "What the hell is that supposed to mean? I married you, didn't I?"

"Please." Shaking her head firmly, she bent to snatch her purse off the floor. Her fingers curled into the leather until her knuckles went white. "You know exactly what I mean. Yes, you married me, but then…nothing. You never wanted to talk about a future. About making a family. Buying a house instead of that condo."

"What the hell was wrong with the condo?"

"Kids need a yard to play in."

"We don't have kids."

"Exactly!" And she'd wanted children. Her own family was so close. Her sisters both had families of their own and Mia's heart had ached to be a mother. But Sam wasn't interested in being a father. He never said so outright, but whenever she'd brought the subject up he'd closed down. She couldn't understand why, either. They'd have made beautiful children together and an amazing life—if only he'd cared enough to fight for their marriage.

"You're talking in circles, Mia." He couldn't look away from the fire in her eyes. Mia Harper was the only woman he'd ever known who could turn from desire to fury to ice and back again in thirty seconds. He'd always loved that about her. She was passionate and proud and so damn bullheaded that even their arguments had been sexy as hell. "Just say whatever it is that's clawing at you."

Shaking her head, she said, "You didn't want children, Sam. And you didn't bother to tell me that until *after* we were married."

True. Sam could admit that silently. Every time Mia had talked about raising a family, he had changed the subject. He'd wanted Mia more than his next breath, but he'd never wanted to be a father. How the hell could he? His own father had sucked at the job, so why would Sam think he would be any better at it? He had hoped that she would change her mind about children. Hoped that he and the life they could have together might be enough for her.

He was wrong.

"What's the point in talking about a future that might not happen?" He took a step closer to her again and he could have sworn he felt heat pumping off her body and this time it was anger, not desire, leading the charge.

"If you don't have a future all you ever have is a past and the present."

"The present can be enough if you're doing it right," he countered.

"Why settle for 'enough' when you can have more?" She stared at him and he saw disappointment in her eyes. He didn't like that but there was little he could do about it.

"How much is more, Mia?" His voice was low, tight. "When do you stop looking for the more and enjoy what you have? Why do you have to walk away from something great because it's missing something else?"

Her posture relaxed a bit and she took a long, deep breath before saying, "I'm tired of being the favorite aunt to Maya's and Merry's kids, Sam. I want children. That's the *more* I need."

He closed off at that because his brain drew up images of Mia, surrounded by nieces and nephews who adored her. Guilt poked at his insides. Sam knew he should have told her that he wasn't interested in having kids before they were married. But he'd wanted her too much to tell her the truth. He'd convinced himself that his lies wouldn't matter once it all ended.

Maybe he had been a bastard. And that was on him. He'd made a choice to have Mia for as long as he could, even knowing that they wouldn't be growing old together. Because he'd wanted her that much, despite knowing in his gut that he wasn't husband material. And how the hell could he be a good father when his father had been so damned bad at the job? Sam's only role model for fatherhood had convinced him to never try it.

"I should have told you," he admitted, though it cost his pride. He wasn't used to being wrong, so he hadn't had to become accustomed to apologies.

"I'm not mad at you about that anymore," she said softly. "We're divorced, Sam. It's over. We don't have to keep tearing at each other over the past."

He gave her a half smile. "But we're not divorced, are we?"

Instantly, she wagged a finger at him. "Oh, no. Don't do that. We may not be divorced, but we're not exactly married, either."

Sam smiled, one corner of his mouth lifting. "Until your new papers go through we are."

"And now you *like* the idea of the two of us married? Why do you care, Sam?" she demanded, pushing her hair back behind one ear to show off a long twist of gold dangling from her lobe. Her eyes shone with a light that was either passion or fury— or maybe a combination of both. "You didn't care when it actually would have mattered."

That slapped at him. Of course he'd cared. It was the only reason he'd tried marriage in the first place.

He'd wanted her. Cared for her. Didn't want to lose her, so marriage had been his only option.

"I did care." He said it simply because if she honestly believed what she was saying, he wanted to convince her she was wrong.

"Really?" She tipped her head to one side and her hair slid off her shoulders to follow the movement. Then she shrugged. "Okay, maybe you did and I just didn't *see* you often enough to notice."

She might have a point, but damned if he'd admit it. He hadn't made a secret of the fact that he *liked* working. That his company was growing and needed close attention paid to it. "You knew when we got married that I run a big company and I work a lot."

Anger drained away and she sighed. "I suppose I did. I just thought that—"

"What?"

"Doesn't matter. Not anymore." Shaking her head, she set the papers down on the nearest tabletop and said, "I'll leave these here. Just call me when you sign them—or even better, have one of your minions bring them to my suite."

He might have smiled at the *minion* remark, but one look into her bruised eyes made that impossible. Whatever had erupted between them only moments before, was gone now. That kiss still burned inside him, but if Mia was feeling the same thing, she was better at hiding emotions than she used to be.

Hell, one of the first things he'd admired about her

was her openness. The way her eyes lit up with pleasure over things most people wouldn't notice at all.

On the cruise when they'd met, she'd tried paddle
boarding for the first time when they were in port
and immediately fell off into the ocean. Sam had
helped her up, thinking she'd be scared or want to
stop and go back to the beach. Instead, she'd come
up from the water laughing, eyes dancing. She'd
climbed back on that board and no matter how many
times she'd fallen off—dozens—she hadn't given
up. Not until she'd found her balance and conquered
that board.

Sam had never had patience for quitters. So
watching this gorgeous woman's stubborn refusal
to give up had appealed to him. Not to mention her
eyes, her laugh, her body, her interest in *everything*.

He'd had an awakening on that cruise a year ago.
Meeting Mia had opened his eyes to a lot of things
he'd stopped noticing years ago. Sunsets. Sunrises.
Pods of whales sailing past the ship. How good it
had felt to sit beside her on the deck and watch the
world drift by.

That's what had drawn him and what had eventually pulled him away. Sam had realized that he and
Mia were too different. Too much opposites to last,
and hanging around longer than he should was only
making it harder on *her*. He wasn't built for cozy.
For *intimate*. Sam Buchanan had been raised to be a
hit-and-run lover. Don't stick around. Don't get close
and for God's sake don't let anyone in.

And nothing had changed, he reminded himself. So he looked into her eyes and nodded. "Fine."

She almost looked disappointed at his response, but he thought he'd imagined that because a heartbeat later, her features were cool and still. Polite and distant. Not something he was accustomed to seeing from Mia. But she was right. The more distance between them the better.

When she left, he didn't watch her go.

"What did he do?" Maya was waiting for Mia on the top deck at a table beneath a red-and-white umbrella.

Mia ignored the question and looked around for her nephews. There were a dozen other passengers gathered on the deck, talking and laughing, and from the deck below came spurts of laughter from excited children. No sign of Charlie and Chris, though. She looked back at her twin. "Where are the kids?"

"You're stalling because you don't want to talk about Sam."

Mia tapped one finger to the end of her nose. "Bingo. So, where are the kids?"

Maya scowled at her. "Joe has them. I think they're throwing snowballs already. And you know I won't quit asking, so just answer already. What did your miserable, no-good ex do?"

Mia groaned. "God, Maya, just stop, okay? You're not making this easier."

"Sorry, sorry." She waved one hand in the air as

if she could erase her words. "Honestly, I'm not try-ing to make things harder for you. It's just that Sam makes me so furious."

"No. Really?"

Maya's lips twitched and Mia grinned. One thing she never had to doubt was her twin's loyalty. When her marriage had fallen apart, leaving Mia in a soggy, weepy, emotional heap, Maya had been there for her. She and their older sister Merry had plied her with bottles of wine and sympathy until Mia had found her feet again.

Her parents had offered support, but had tried to maintain neutrality and though that might seem like a betrayal of sorts to someone else, Mia had appreciated it. Sam wasn't an evil person. Not the Darth Vader of Seal Beach. He just hadn't wanted to be married.

"Okay." Maya picked up her virgin mimosa and signaled to a nearby waiter to bring another for Mia. "Let's rephrase. How did your most wonderful ex take the news?"

Mia gave her a wry smile, then thanked the waiter who handed her a beautiful crystal flute. "Let's not go too far the other way." She paused, thought about it, then said, "He was…surprised."

"Well, yeah. Who wasn't?" Shaking her head, Maya sat back in her chair. "I still can't believe peo-ple weren't complaining about not getting their pack-ages delivered. How does a delivery driver become a hoarder with other people's stuff?"

"I don't know. And it doesn't matter now anyway," Mia said. "All I need is for Sam to sign the papers so I can get the divorce filed before January 15th."

"So he didn't sign them." Maya nodded sagely.

"Not yet," Mia agreed. "But he will."

"And you know this how?"

"Because he didn't fight the divorce, remember?" That still stung whether Mia wanted to admit it or not. When she'd first broached the subject of divorce it had taken everything she'd had. She'd prepared herself for his arguments. For his request for a second chance. But she needn't have bothered. He didn't argue. Didn't really say much at all.

She could still see his face in her memory. Standing opposite her in the living room of the condo they shared, he'd simply stared at her, his features blank and hard—as if he'd been carved out of stone. When he finally spoke, all he'd said was, "If that's what you want, I won't stop you."

Well, she'd *wanted* him to stop her. Wanted him to admit that he hadn't given their marriage a real shot. That he'd been wrong to shut himself off from her.

Instead, she'd gotten an uncontested divorce.

"Damn it," Maya blurted, snapping Mia out of her depressing thoughts. "I hate this. I hate seeing shadows back in your eyes. You were finally okay. Moving on without him. Planning a life and a future and now you're right back where you started a few months ago."

"Stop being so dramatic," Mia said and took a sip

of her drink. "I'm not going to throw myself off the ship. This is just a bump in my formerly tidy world."

Maya narrowed her eyes on Mia and studied her until Mia shifted uncomfortably beneath that knowing stare.

"Why are you looking at me like that?"

"Because you're right. You *are* fine. And I want to know why." Leaning forward, she kept their gazes locked. "You weren't there long enough to have sex with him."

"Maya!" Mia glanced around to make sure no one else had overheard her sister.

"Well, come on. Even distracted by kids, a house payment and his job, Joe can last longer than twenty minutes."

"Too much information, thanks. Now I'll have that in my head when I see Joe next."

"I know envy when I hear it," Maya said with a grin.

Mia snorted a laugh and took another sip.

"But there's something different about you. Something…" Suddenly Maya's eyes snapped. "You kissed him. Didn't you?"

No point in denying it. Maya had always had X-ray vision when it came to things like this. For a moment, Mia pitied her nephews when they became teenagers. They'd never put one over on their mother.

"He kissed me," Mia finally said. "There's a difference."

"And you fought him off, of course," Maya supplied wryly.

"Desperately," Mia assured her, then set her glass down with a click on the glass table. "Fine. I kissed him back."

Maya huffed a breath in disgust. "I knew this would happen."

The sun shone out of a sky so blue it hurt to look at it. A sharp, cold wind brushed past them, setting the fringe on the red-and-white umbrellas snapping and dancing.

"Wow, you're wasting time working at the family bakery. You should be on the Psychic Network or something."

Maya smirked at her. "Please. Like I have to be a fortune teller to know that you'd fall back into his arms."

"Okay," Mia said, defending herself, "I didn't do that. It was a kiss. And I ended it."

"Before or after he got your shirt off?"

"Maya!" Mia goggled at her sister. As twins, they were close. As best friends, they knew each other way too well, so she wasn't surprised at Maya, so much as disappointed in herself. She had pretty much given in to the urge to kiss Sam again. But why wouldn't she? Just because they were divorced didn't mean she'd stopped loving him.

Just because Mia knew she could gain ten pounds just by *looking* at chocolate cake didn't mean she'd stop eating it.

"I managed to keep my clothes on, thanks for your support."

"Oh, you have my support, honey. But trust me, I know what's going on between you two." She patted her baby bump. "Remember. I'm on number three child. Every time Joe walks into the room, I want to jump him. Heck, at this rate, I'm going to have ten kids. So believe me when I say I understand."

Mia sighed a little and quashed that twinge of envy she felt for her sister's life. Maya's husband was a firefighter and their two boys, Charlie and Chris, were funny, ferocious and all around adorable. Now Maya was pregnant with another boy and Mia knew that in a year or two, her twin would be trying for a girl again.

Maya had everything that Mia most wanted. She had love. Family. Children of her own. It's what Mia had hoped for when she'd married Sam. Building a life together. Raising some kids together.

But Sam hadn't really wanted children. Naturally, she hadn't believed him when he told her on their honeymoon. She'd wrongly assumed that he had simply never been around kids, so didn't know how much fun—okay yes, and trouble—they could be. And maybe he would have changed his mind at some point—if their marriage had lasted. But now she'd never know.

"But jumping Sam won't change anything," Maya said and thankfully her voice was low, soft.

"Yeah, I know that." Didn't stop her from *want-*

ing to jump him, but she was stronger than her hormones. She hoped.

"Honey, once he signs those damn papers, you can pick up your life again."

"I know that too, Maya," she said tightly.

Her twin must have caught the fine edge of tension in Mia's voice because she said, "Fine, fine. I'll stop."

"Hallelujah."

"Funny. Let's see if you're still laughing after you spend the day with my kids."

"Your kids are great," Mia argued.

"Yeah, they are," Maya said. "But don't tell them I said that." She scooted her chair back and held one hand out. "Now, help your prego twin out of this stupid chair, will you? I've got to figure out where I'm going to put that Christmas elf in our suite."

Mia laughed and pulled her twin out of the chair. "You brought Buddy the Elf with you?"

"Of course I did." Maya threw her hands up. "Both boys look for him the instant they wake up in the morning. And they know that Buddy reports to Santa so..." She shrugged. "It seemed like a good way to keep the boys in line while we're on this cruise."

"Uh-huh."

Maya gave her a hard look. "Just wait until it's your turn to hide that elf and you have to find a new spot every day!"

Mia could hardly wait.

* * *

For the next couple of hours, Sam buried himself in work. It was the best way. Always his answer to avoiding emotional issues, he'd been doing it since he was a kid.

Back then, his father had made it clear that a man's duty was to take care of his business and his employees. Emotions were something to be *avoided*. He would point out that marrying Sam and Mike's mother had been the biggest mistake of his life, since he'd had to settle an enormous sum on her when they divorced. He considered his sons to be his only compensation for his relationship with their mother.

His father had always demanded that Sam *think*. That he never allow his feelings, whatever they might be, to rule any decisions made. Well, Sam had broken that decree when he'd married Mia. He'd allowed emotion to swamp his judgment and now he was paying for it. He'd taken the risk—and lost.

"You're not getting any work done," he muttered and tossed his pen onto the desk in front of him.

Avoiding Mia wasn't going to do him any good if he couldn't get her out of his mind. He stared out at the ocean, letting his brain wander, hoping it would come up with a strategy for how to deal with this.

Deal.

At the thought of that word, Sam's brain leaped back to the idea that had occurred to him earlier. He'd dismissed it at first of course, because he might be a bastard, but was he low enough to actually black-mail Mia?

Slowly, his gaze slid to the envelope Mia had left behind when she walked out of the suite.

Divorce papers.

He hadn't signed them yet.

And he wasn't sure why.

He wasn't holding onto the past. He'd already come to grips with the end of their marriage. But she was here now, he reminded himself. She wanted those papers signed and he had to wonder what she'd be willing to do to see that happen.

A knock on the door had Sam's head snapping up. Mia? Come back to...what? Was she looking to expand on that kiss that was still sending sparks sizzling through him? His body responded to that thought with a rush of heat that staggered him.

He walked to the door, yanked it open and the heat instantly drained away.

"Hi, Uncle Sam!" Charlie Rossi, Maya's five-year-old son, raced past him into the suite and on his heels was his three-year-old brother, Chris. Chris didn't say much, but he waved in passing.

"Hey you guys, don't run!" Joe Rossi, their father and Sam's brother-in-law shouted, then turned to Sam and held out one hand. "Good to see you."

"Yeah," he said, shaking the man's hand. "You too. And surprising."

He'd expected that Mia's family was onboard just to throw stones at him and protect Mia from him.

He hadn't been prepared to see a friendly face in the bunch.

"I'll bet." Joe walked past him, looked for his sons and relaxed a little when he saw them jumping onto the couch. "Stop jumping, that's not your trampoline."

Chris stopped instantly. Charlie was a harder sell. "Uncle Sam, Dad says we can have a snowball war if we're good and don't bug you so do you have cookies?"

"What?" Sam looked at the boy, whose sun-streaked brown hair was dipping into green eyes much like his mother's. "Uh, no. I don't have cookies."

"Juice box?" Chris asked.

"No, sorry." He hadn't expected to be entertaining kids. And his features must have said so, because Joe came to his rescue.

"Relax you guys, you just ate lunch." Joe walked to the couch, picked up a TV remote and said, "Here. Watch that cartoon movie you like so much while I talk to Uncle Sam."

"Okay," Charlie agreed happily enough, dropping onto the couch hard enough to make his little brother bounce and fall over. "Then snowball war?"

"Yeah," Joe said. "If you're good."

"Be good, Chris," Charlie warned.

"Right," Joe muttered, with a laugh, "because he's the problem." Glancing at Sam, he added, "Should feel bad about that," he confessed. "Using the TV for a babysitter, I mean."

Sam watched Joe with his sons and thought how differently the Rossi kids were being raised than Sam had been. Hell, if he'd jumped up and down on a sofa, his father would have hit the roof.

Shaking his head, he pushed all of that aside and asked, "Want some coffee?" Sam asked. "And I've got water and probably sodas in the wet bar if the kids—"

"I'll take the caffeine," Joe said quickly, "and pass on it for the kids, but thanks. They're fine."

"Okay." Sam led the way to the coffee station along one wall and poured each of them a cup. "So, I saw Maya…"

Joe winced. "She's not real happy with you."

"Yeah, that was pretty clear." He could still see Mia's sister glaring at him like he was Jack the Ripper or something.

"The thing is," Joe said cautiously, "most of us aren't."

Sam didn't like hearing that and it surprised him. But Sam had always liked Joe, and Merry's husband Alan and Mia's parents, too. Of course, he'd known going into the marriage that it probably wasn't going to work out, so he hadn't gotten close to any of them. But still, they were good people.

"I can understand that," he admitted, and took a sip of coffee. "What I don't get is why you're all here on this cruise."

"Seriously?" Joe snorted a laugh, drank his coffee then shot a look at his sons, completely wrapped up in some movie apparently starring some weird-looking snowman. Turning his gaze back to Sam, he said, "You should know the Harper family well enough to know that when one of them's in trouble, they circle the wagons."

"Against me."

"Pretty much."

Nodding, Sam said, "Fine. But this is still between Mia and me."

"You'd think so, but no." Shaking his head, Joe continued, "Whatever happens between you two affects everything else. It's family, Sam."

On an intellectual level, Sam got it. But otherwise, no. He hadn't grown up with anything like the Harper family. He was taught to stand on his own—*don't let anyone close and if they do get past your walls, shut down so they can't affect you.*

He'd learned those lessons well. Sam had taken a risk, gone against everything he'd believed and married Mia even knowing it would all come crashing down. If he had regrets, they were his own. And he wasn't going to bare his soul for the Harper family, either.

"If you're here to push me into signing those papers, you didn't have to bother," Sam said.

"Yeah, that's not why I'm here." He broke off, glared at his son and said, "Charlie, I said no bouncing on the furniture." Looking at Sam again, he said, "My wife is pretty pissed at you."

"Yeah. I know."

"What you don't know is I don't agree with her." He held up one hand and added, "And if you tell her I said that, I'll claim you're a liar."

"Okay…" This was as unexpected as the surprise visit.

"You screwed up."

"Thanks." Sam lifted his coffee cup in a silent toast.

"No problem," Joe said amiably. "But the thing is, one screw-up doesn't have to end everything. You and Mia were good together. And hell, I like you."

Sam laughed shortly. "Thanks."

"So I'm thinking you shouldn't sign the papers. At least not right away." Joe shrugged, shot his bouncing son another warning look, then continued, "What the hell, Sam. You've got a two-week cruise. Use it. Talk to Mia. Figure out what the hell went wrong and maybe you can fix it."

Sam already knew what had gone wrong. And talking about it wouldn't change a damn thing. He just wasn't husband material. Probably never would be. How could he be? His own father had sucked at all four of his brief marriages and then had spent the next thirty years bouncing from one temporary woman to the next. Not exactly a sterling role model.

There were lots of things Sam wanted to do with Mia, but talking wasn't one of them.

"I appreciate the moral support, Joe. Seriously. But I don't think this is salvageable."

"Huh." Joe looked at him. "Never pegged you as a quitter."

Insulted, he said, "Yeah, I'm not."

"Could have fooled me."

Sam laughed again. "First a pep talk, then insults?"

Joe shrugged again. "Whatever works, man." He set his coffee cup down. "Look. Up to you, but you're both on this boat anyway. Might as well make the most of it, don't you think?"

Sam frowned thoughtfully, and realized that what Joe was saying almost lined up with his idea about making a deal with Mia. Probably not what the other man had had in mind, but it did slide right in there.

Joe wasn't waiting for an answer. He'd already turned to his kids. "All right you two! Snow time!"

"Yay!" Charlie jumped off the couch and his shadow, Chris, was right behind him. "Bye, Uncle Sam!" he shouted as he headed for the door.

"Bye!" Chris echoed, following his big brother.

"See you around, Sam..." Joe lifted one hand, then led his kids out the door. Before he closed it behind him though, he said, "Think about it. Talk to Mia. What've you got to lose?"

The TV was still on and some silly song was rolling through the suite. Sam didn't hear it. Instead, he was thinking about what Joe had said and wondering if he should give in to what he wanted—or just let Mia have the ending she was asking for.

Four

Make the most of it.

Sam snorted as he told himself that Joe probably hadn't meant his advice in the same way Sam was taking it. But for the next two weeks, Sam and Mia would be stranded on this ship. And the *Fantasy Nights* wasn't big enough for them to be able to ignore each other for long.

"And why should we?" Frowning, he stared down at the deck below, watching his employees working with the passengers, laughing, talking, making everyone at home.

But while he studied the small crowd, his mind was on Mia. Not married. Not divorced. So didn't that clear the way for them to be whatever the hell they wanted to be?

And that begged the question—what exactly *did* Sam want?

That was easy. He wanted Mia. Always had. Since the first time he'd seen her, all he'd been able to think of was getting her alone. Getting her into the nearest bed and keeping her there. That hadn't changed.

Their marriage had been a mistake, no doubt. But that failure hadn't killed his desire for her. He didn't think that was possible.

They could have two weeks together. Sam wouldn't promise her forever. Not again. But he could give her now.

Of course the moment that thought registered, he remembered that Mia had accused him of only considering the "now." But hell, that's all any of them were promised, right? There was no guarantee of tomorrow and yesterday was already gone. So why not focus on *now*?

All he had to do was bring her around to that same realization. He scowled as he acknowledged that wasn't going to be easy. But maybe, if she couldn't be convinced, he could try a little friendly blackmail.

She could move into his suite for the duration of the cruise—and he'd sign her divorce papers.

No. Though everything in him wanted to, damned if he wanted Mia back in his bed because she thought she had no choice. Scowling he was forced to admit that there were some lines he wasn't prepared to cross.

* * *

"Why did you bring the elf with you?" Mia shook her head as she watched her twin stalk around their suite.

"My choice was…what? Admit he's not real?" Maya gave her a hard look. "Want me to tell the boys Santa's not real, too?"

"Of course not." Mia loved those kids like her own and seeing their excitement for Christmas and Santa was wonderful. She couldn't wait to experience it all for herself with her own children.

"Well then, Buddy has to be here." Maya frowned to herself. "You know, he reports to Santa every night on the boys' behavior. Using that as extortion is the one chance I have to make sure they don't destroy this boat while we're on it."

Mia laughed. "They're not monsters, Maya."

Her twin smiled. "No. But they are little kids with too much Christmas excitement rattling around inside them and it's bound to erupt at some point. Buddy the Elf is my only hope to keep it contained."

"And you have to do this right now?" Mia leaned back into the navy blue couch, propped her feet on the coffee table in front of her and said, "We've only been onboard ship for a couple of hours. What's the rush?"

Maya sighed and laid her forearm on the crest of her sizable baby bump. "Because Joe's got the boys out exploring, so I want to take the opportunity to look for elf places while I can."

"Fine. I'll help."

"It needs to be easy enough for the kids to find him in the morning. And I'll need a few of them, to last over the whole trip." Maya frowned and shook her head. "I can reuse the spots of course, the kids are so little, they won't really pay attention. But I'm going to need at least three or four." She turned that frown on her twin. "When you said you'd help, did you mean today?"

Mia laughed. "Jeez, you're crabby when you're pregnant."

"You try having a tiny human jumping up and down on your bladder like it's a trampoline and see what kind of mood you're in." A moment later, Maya groaned. "I'm sorry honey."

"It's okay."

"No," Maya said, "it's really not. I'm not really mad. Just…tense. I guess I'm still worried about Joe. He was so tired when he got back from that Idaho wildfire."

"He looks good now," Mia said and knew her sister would worry anyway. Joe and several others had flown from their fire station in Seal Beach to Idaho to help fight a fast-spreading wildfire. And for the five days he was gone, Maya had hardly slept. So it wasn't just Joe who needed this trip to relax and catch up on some sleep.

"He does." Maya nodded firmly. "And I'm probably overreacting—hormonal and all."

"And you love Joe."

"I do."

"So..." Mia stood up and forced a smile. "Let's find some hiding spots for Buddy and then go sit on the deck so you can relax a little."

"That sounds great."

Mia looked around the suite. There were two bedrooms. Joe, Maya and the boys had one and Mia had the other. And the living area was a good size, so they could surely find someplace to hide an elf.

"Oh," Maya said, "you should know that Dad says he's going to talk to Sam."

"Great," Mia said on a sigh. "That'll go well."

"Oh come on. Dad won't hurt him," Maya said. "Much."

Mia sat down again. "Maybe it was a bad idea bringing all of you guys along on this cruise."

"Thanks a bunch," Maya said, opening a cabinet door and shutting it again. "I feel so special now."

"You know what I mean. Backup is one thing," Mia said, "but I didn't want you all to be an attack squad."

"God, drama queen." Maya laughed. "Nobody's attacking Sam. Yet," she added with a grin. "We just sort of want him to know what he lost."

"Well, if you have to *tell* him what he lost, what's the point?"

"To irritate him, of course." Maya walked across the room and dropped carefully onto the closest chair. Her smile faded and she looked at her twin with sympathy. "Sweetie, we're on your side. We won't do anything you don't want us to. We just want to be here so Sam can't crush you again."

Her head snapped back and she winced at the description. "I wasn't crushed."

"Please." Maya's eyes rolled.

"Fine." She had been destroyed when her marriage ended. But she'd mourned what might have been more than what *had* been. Because if she were honest with herself, the marriage itself hadn't been worth her tears. She'd been alone for the most part and even when Sam was home, she felt as if she were the only one in the room.

He'd managed to be close to her and as distant as the moon all at the same time. It was as if the moment they got married, Sam had turned inward, shutting her out. The worst part was, she didn't know *why*. And probably never would.

"You're right. It was bad at first. The difference is, now I won't be crushed."

"And how're you going to prevent it?" Maya watched her and Mia thought that sometimes she really hated how her sister knew her so well.

"Because I won't let myself. I learned my lesson. I'm not going to believe in Sam again."

Maya continued to study her silently for several long seconds, then finally nodded. "Okay then. I'm going to hold you to that."

"Go ahead. In fact," Mia said suddenly, "I'll bet you twenty bucks that I'll leave this cruise Sam-free and my heart in one glorious piece."

That wasn't entirely true and Mia knew it. Just thinking about Sam brought up images of them together in her mind. She felt the heat of the flames licking at her blood and the ache inside her only grew. The next two weeks, being so close to Sam was going to be the hardest thing she'd ever done.

But any pain she felt…this time she would hide it from the family and instead bury it so deep within that she'd never really have to face it herself.

Quickly, her twin said, "I'll take that bet."

"Thanks for your support," Mia said wryly.

"Hey, twenty bucks is twenty bucks." Maya sighed a little. "And the truth is, Sam is your Kryptonite."

"He used to be," Mia corrected, ignoring the memory of the blast of heat that had seared her during that kiss she'd shared with him. She wouldn't allow him to be that important to her again.

Mia had plans for her life. And to make sure those plans came to reality, she had to get Sam to sign those divorce papers. Keeping that thought firmly in mind would see her survive this cruise without letting her heart drop into Sam's lap.

"Well," Maya said, "now that we have that settled, do you think it would send the wrong message if Buddy was hidden in the liquor cabinet?"

Laughing, Mia pushed thoughts of Sam out of her mind and concentrated on the magical elf instead. At least for the moment.

The next day, Sam met with Kira Anderson, the navigation officer, on the prow of the ship. Out there, with only the wind and the sound of the sea slapping against the hull, Sam fought to concentrate as she walked him through the latest weather reports.

"It looks as though we might catch a break," she was saying as she pointed to the graphic she'd printed out. "The storm isn't a big one, and it's moving at a pretty good clip. About a half hour ago, it shifted position here, heading further out of our path." She pointed to one of the red lines on the paper. "There's still a chance it will swing around and be waiting for us. But right now, it looks as though we'll miss it."

Sam studied the paper she handed him. Only their second day at sea and already a storm was brewing. Both on and off the ship, he thought wryly. Hell, with Mia here, everything had shifted and Sam was still trying to find his sea legs. He hadn't slept the night before, because every time he closed his eyes, he saw Mia. That kiss was still lingering on his lips and the burn she engendered in him had him feeling as though he was on fire.

Shaking his head, he pushed those thoughts aside and looked at Kira. "And what if we don't miss it? How big a storm are we talking about?"

She considered that for a moment and looked out at the ocean as if looking for confirmation before turning back to him. "Nothing that could endanger the ship or passengers, sir. But it could make the ship's doctor really busy doling out seasick pills."

His lips twitched. Didn't matter what time of year they were sailing, there was always going to be at least one night when the waves were high, and the winds strong enough to turn even the most practiced sailor into a whimpering shadow of himself, praying for death.

"All right," he finally said, handing back the papers. "Monitor closely and keep me in the loop about what you're expecting."

"Yes, sir." She practically saluted before turning to head back to the bridge.

"And Kira," he called out and waited for her to stop and turn to him before adding, "I want to know your best prediction by seven. Let's give our guests time to prepare. I don't want anyone unnecessarily scared over this."

"Understood." She nodded and hurried away.

Alone again, Sam thought about the possible storm and scowled to himself. He wasn't worried about what might happen. Sam had been sailing all of his life and faced the worst storm he'd seen before or since when he was fourteen.

He'd taken his skiff out alone, wanting to escape a house that had felt like a prison. Sam had been sailing for two hours when the clouds rolled in. Lightning punched the sky, rain fell as if it'd been poured from an upturned bucket. Fear was a living thing inside him.

Visibility was so bad he didn't know which way the shore was and he knew that one wrong decision and his boat would be pushed out into the open ocean with chances of a rescue slim. But he couldn't do nothing, either. The waves had battered his small boat until he was sure it would fall apart.

So he made a decision and headed toward what he hoped was the shore. He was out there, in the storm, alone, for what felt like years, though it was only an hour before he landed on the beach, exhausted, wet and cold.

By the time he'd walked home, it was late and his father was waiting. The old man didn't want to hear about the storm. He said Sam was irresponsible. He didn't deserve a damn boat and he wouldn't be getting another one. And if he didn't know enough to stay out of the ocean during a storm, he'd send Sam to a private school in the desert. Dear old dad had made it clear that night, just how low Sam was on his list of priorities.

But if one good thing had happened that night—besides surviving that storm—Sam had finally accepted that his father didn't give a damn about him. He was on his own and the sooner he stopped waiting for someone to care, the easier it would be. The memory faded away and Sam realized his hands were fisted around the iron railing. Deliberately, he relaxed his grip.

"Yeah," he muttered now. "Hell of a role model, Dad."

Shutting off the ancient images in his mind, he looked down at the pool deck. There were kids everywhere of course, with the ship lifeguards on red alert. Adults strolled the deck, huddled by the pool bar or tried to lounge in the water in spite of the splashing and shrieking coming from the kids.

The sky was blue and dense with heavy white clouds. Waves crested and fell across the surface of the water and made Sam wonder if they were closing in on that storm faster than Kira had thought.

Then Sam spotted Mia's parents. He took a breath and let it out again as he studied the couple. They were at a rail, staring out over the ocean. At five foot ten, Henry Harper was a good six inches taller than his wife, Emma. He had his right arm draped across his wife's shoulders and she was leaning into his embrace. A unit. That's how Sam had seen them from the beginning. They could have been alone in the world instead of on a cruise ship filled with Christmas-hyped kids.

And a part of Sam envied them their unity. The Harpers had welcomed him into their family when he married Mia. But he seriously doubted whether that welcome was still alive and well. Actually, he knew it wasn't. Knew that when he left Mia, the Harper family had left *him*.

Yet they were here, on his boat and trying to avoid them for the next couple of weeks would be ridiculous.

"Besides," he muttered as he headed for the closest staircase that would take him to the pool deck, "they should be thanking me." Staying married to Mia would have been a disaster. By leaving, he'd spared her a hell of a lot of pain further down the road.

"Sure. They're going to believe that," he said to himself. Hell, even he had a hard time with it.

Sam walked a wide berth around the pool area, then headed for the Harpers. As if sensing his approach, Henry turned his head and pinned Sam with a cold stare.

Sam kept walking, though it felt as though he was making his way through a minefield. When he was close enough, he said, "Hello Henry, Emma."

Henry nodded. Emma didn't so much as twitch. It was as if Sam was invisible to her.

The sun was bright, the wind was cold and the air was filled with the kind of noise only twenty or thirty kids could make.

"Sam," Henry said, giving him a brief nod. The man's reddish-brown hair whipped in the wind and the green eyes he'd passed on to his daughters focused on Sam. "Didn't expect to see you."

"Really? I thought that was why you'd come on this trip with Mia. To see me."

"No." Henry shook his head. "We're here to make sure you don't hurt our girl again. That's all."

Sam gritted his teeth against that verbal slap because he respected Henry. He wouldn't argue with the older man, and how could he? He *had* hurt Mia. But he'd hurt her far less than he might have if they'd been married longer.

He glanced at Emma, who hadn't once shifted her gaze from the ocean to him. Sighing, he turned his gaze back to Henry. "Okay then. I won't keep you.

I only wanted to let you know, we may be heading into a storm later."

Henry took a brief look at the sunny sky and the water, choppy, but hardly threatening, before saying, "Is your boat up to it?"

Sam laughed shortly and tucked both hands into his pockets. "Every one of the Buchanan boats are built for stability as well as comfort."

"Stability," Emma repeated.

Sam's gaze switched to her, but she wasn't looking at him. Frowning a bit, he said to Henry, "We'll be safe, but it could be a rough night."

Henry looked around at the people enjoying the day, then said, "You're not telling the other passengers?"

"We will, later. If it looks as though we can't avoid the storm." Sam winced when a wet beach ball smacked the middle of his back. Looking over his shoulder, he saw a young boy hurry after the ball before heading back to the pool. Focusing on Henry again, he said, "I didn't see the point in worrying everyone until we knew for sure."

"But you didn't mind worrying us?"

"That's not what I meant." Of course, that's how Henry would see it. But the truth was, Henry was a coolheaded person and wasn't inclined toward panic. "I knew you weren't the kind of man to overreact."

"Uh-huh." Henry watched him. "Think you know me, do you?"

Confused and a little wary, Sam said, "Yes. I do."

"Well," Henry told him, "I once thought I knew you. But I was wrong. So you might be as well."

"Henry—" Sam didn't know what he could say. Hell, what he wanted to say. But it felt as though he should be trying, somehow.

"No," the older man said, dropping his arm from Emma's shoulders. "I didn't get my say when all this blew up. You just walked out on my daughter and acted like the rest of us didn't exist."

"I figured you wouldn't want to see me."

"You weren't wrong."

Sam really didn't want this confrontation, but there was no way to avoid it now. Thankfully, with the crowd around the pool, the noise level was high enough that it would keep anyone else from listening in. Pulling his hands free of his pockets, Sam folded his arms across his chest and met Henry's gaze straight on. "Mia asked me for a divorce. I gave her one."

"And why'd she need that divorce, Sam?" Henry tipped his head to one side and stared at him. "Could it be because you didn't mind having a wedding, but you really didn't want to be married?"

That skimmed a little too close to home. "I'm not getting into any of it, Henry. That's between me and Mia."

"You making my girl cry over you?" Henry countered. "That makes it my business, too."

She'd cried. Of course she had. Sam hadn't let himself think about that because he just couldn't take the image of a teary Mia. Especially knowing it was his fault. If he'd never married her, none of this would be happening.

But he'd been so blinded by desire—by feelings he'd never known before, he hadn't been able to stop himself even when he knew he was risking disaster for both of them. Sam had known that Mia wasn't a 'temporary' kind of woman and so he'd tried. He'd taken that risk because he'd wanted her so badly. Hell, he still wanted Mia more than his next breath. She was the only woman who had ever tempted him to try marriage. And look where it had gotten them both.

Still, it was over and done now. Everybody should be moving the hell on. Sounded great, he thought. But he wasn't thinking about moving on. He was focused on finding Mia and kissing her senseless. Letting himself feel the burn of her touch and the rushing slide into a heat he'd only found with her. Shaking his head, he let go of those thoughts and looked at his in-laws.

"Look, Henry," he said, done trying to apologize for doing the right thing. As a husband, he was a failure. Should he have stuck around long enough that Mia was begging him to leave? "I can't change your opinion of me and frankly, I'm not going to try. I only wanted to give you and your family a heads-up about the possible storm. Now that I have, I'll leave you to enjoy yourselves."

It looked as though Henry had more to say, but

instead, he smashed his lips together as if locking the words inside. But before he could go, Sam heard Emma speaking.

"You know something Henry," she said, still watching the water as if she were mesmerized, "if Sam were here, I'd tell him what a disappointment he is to me."

Sam felt that sting down to his bones. Emma had always been good to him. He'd seen her relationship with her daughters and it had been a revelation to him. He'd never known a *real* family dynamic and he'd liked it. Enjoyed it. He was accepted as a son—much like Joe and Merry's husband, Alan. He hadn't even known how much that had meant to him until it was gone.

Now, Emma wouldn't look at him.

"Emma—" he started.

"And," she continued, "I'd tell him if he hurts my baby again, the storm won't be his only problem."

There was nothing he could say to turn things around, so Sam just kept quiet.

Emma looked up at Henry and said, "Let's take a walk, shall we?"

Henry gave him a brief look, then nodded at his wife. "Sure. Let's go check on the kids in the snow room."

"That'll be fun," Emma said and walked past Sam as if he were a ghost.

And to her, he told himself, that's exactly what

he was. The ghost of a man who'd made promises
he didn't keep.

Sam watched them go, then stabbed one hand
through his hair. When his marriage to Mia had
ended, so had everything else. He'd tried to be nice to
Henry and Emma. They weren't interested. So why
should he keep trying to be Mr. Nice Guy? This was
his ship. His world. They were only passing through.

Being here with Mia was a gift from the universe. The fires between them were still burning. He
still ached to have her with him and now he had his
chance. Once, he'd married her because the desperate need inside him had demanded it—and he'd let
her go because she'd needed him to. Now he needed
and damned if he'd waste this opportunity. And once
this cruise was over, they'd go back to reality and
never have to see each other again.

So maybe it was time to rethink that "deal" he'd
considered earlier. A nice guy wouldn't do it. But
apparently, that wasn't who he was.

And that opened up a world of possibilities.

Mia spent most of the day in the ship's kitchen.
She knew several of the chefs from her time with
Sam and it was good to see them all. But she acknowledged, at least to herself, that the real reason
she was in the kitchen, was that it was literally the
last place on earth she had to worry about running
into Sam.

The Buchanan ships were small enough that it

wasn't easy to hide—it would have been much easier to disappear into a crowd of thousands on the bigger cruise ships.

Chefs were moving about the kitchen as if they were in a well-rehearsed dance. Miles of stainless steel countertops were stacked with dishes being readied for the dining room and a dozen conversations were happening at once.

"This is great, Mia." Holly Chambers, pastry chef on the *Fantasy Nights*, was barely five feet tall and wore her black hair cut close to her head. Her blue eyes were always bright and smiling and a pair of gold studs were in her ears. When Mia and Holly had met a year ago, they'd bonded over baking.

The Harper family bakery, Your Daily Bread, specialized in…naturally, bread. But as Mia and her sisters took over more of the bakery, they were growing the menu, too. Now they offered Italian cookies, English scones, cannoli, sticky toffee pudding and a tiramisu that could bring tears of joy to your eyes.

But today, Mia was showing Holly how to make her mother's amazing rosemary bread. As she kneaded the fragrant dough on the stainless steel counter, Mia said, "This is one of the best sellers at the bakery."

"I'm loving it already and it hasn't been baked yet," Holly said, checking her notes to make sure she'd written the recipe down perfectly.

Mia smiled to herself. This was therapeutic to her.

Kneading dough, creating something amazing out of flour and herbs.

"Oh, and it smells like heaven when it's baking," Mia said. If there was one thing the Harper kids knew, it was baking. All three of her parents' daughters had started working at the bakery when they were kids. They'd grown up around the ovens, the proving room where yeast breads rose, and the front of the shop where customers lined up every morning to buy the day's special.

Mia's mom's family was Italian and English, which explained why their dessert menu was so eclectic. The Harper sisters had grown up making those treats and experimenting with new dishes.

Now, the sisters had serious plans for growth. Not only to open another bakery, but they wanted to start a traditional British tea shop as well.

But that was still down the road, Mia thought. She had her life to straighten out first and she couldn't move forward with any of those plans until she'd put her marriage—and Sam—behind her.

And *that* thought brought up an instant wave of heat.

Ridiculous, that a simple turn of phrase "put Sam behind her" could remind her of all those times she'd *had* Sam behind her. Her breathing quickened and she told herself to stop it. Already, she was working on very little sleep because her dreams had been filled with Sam. Memories crowded into her mind, forcing her to remember not just the pain, but the joy, the passion, the—

Okay, cut it out.

She punched the dough down a little more vigorously than required, and automatically began patting it into a domed circle.

Lost in her thoughts, Mia jumped when beside her, Holly called out, "Oh, hi, Mr. Buchanan."

"Oh, God," Mia murmured.

Five

He was watching her, his gaze fixed, his expression unreadable.

Mia took a breath, but it didn't stop her heart from jumping in her chest, or her blood from turning into steam in her veins. He wore a suit, of course. Navy blue, tailored to perfection, with a white dress shirt and a red tie. Cruise to Hawaii or not, Sam Buchanan was the picture of business elegance, with a touch of pirate, since his hair was a little too long.

Had she conjured Sam simply by thinking about him? No, that couldn't be true, or he would have been appearing in her apartment constantly over the last few months. He'd been the center of her thoughts since the day they'd met and even going through a divorce hadn't ended that.

Mia looked up and saw him, standing just inside the kitchen, watching her. Second day of the cruise and already she was seeing him way too often for her own good. How was she going to make it through two whole weeks?

"Hello Holly," he said, then added, "Mia."

The rest of the kitchen staff simply went about their business. They were busy prepping for dinner, so no one had time to talk—well, except for Holly. Her pastries wouldn't be part of the amazing on-board menu until morning and the breakfast buffet.

Mia said, "Hello, Sam," then turned back to the rosemary dough. "You can bake it in a simple round, like this," she told Holly, "or, you can actually divide it into three, braid it and then draw the ends into a circle. Not only is it delicious, but it makes for a gorgeous presentation."

"I'm convinced," Holly said with a grin.

"Once it's risen," Mia said, "bake it for about a half hour at 375 until it's nice and golden."

"Got it." Holly tossed a glance at Sam again and Mia could see she was a little tense with her boss standing there watching.

Mia knew just how she felt.

"Let me know how it turns out," Mia said and patted Holly's arm. Then she walked toward Sam and his gaze narrowed on her as she got closer. It was as if the hundreds of kitchen workers didn't exist.

She and Sam saw only each other. She wished she was wearing something more impressive than a simple pair of white shorts and a bright yellow, scoop-necked T-shirt. Her hair was pulled into a ponytail and she wore a pair of black sneakers that were now dusted with flour. Damn it. He looked like an ad in *GQ* and she looked…well, like *her*.

She could have sworn she actually felt her skin sizzle under that stare of his. But she wouldn't let him know it. She stopped right in front of him and keeping her voice low, said, "You're making Holly and probably everyone else in here a little nervous."

One eyebrow winged up and he shot a quick look around the room as if to see for himself that she was right. Shrugging, he said, "I didn't come here for them. I came to talk to you."

"How'd you know I was here?" And she'd thought her hiding place would see her through this cruise.

"It's my ship, Mia," he said, his gaze boring into hers. "I know everything that happens on it."

"Right." Someone had tipped him off. How nice to be a god in your own little world. She sighed. "Okay, you found me. Let's take this somewhere else, all right?"

Mia headed out the door and into the main dining hall. Scores of tables were set up, each of them covered in pristine white cloths. Waiters were already hustling around the room, setting up carafes of ice water while others placed water and wineglasses at every setting.

She didn't have to look behind her to know he was hot on her heels. Mia *sensed* his presence. The man was a force of nature. At least that's how it had always seemed to Mia. Her very own, personal Category 5 hurricane.

He had swept into her life and turned everything upside down. And even when he had left her, there was rubble in his wake.

Through another door and they were outside on Deck Two and the wind slapped at her. Mia turned her face into the cold, salty sting of it, hoping it would clear her mind. She walked to the railing, looked out at the choppy sea, then turned to Sam as he moved up beside her.

"Why were you looking for me?"

"Just wanted to talk to you."

"The papers?" she asked. "Did you sign them?"

"No."

She sighed again. Why was he making this so much harder than it had to be? "Fine. What is it, then?"

"Wanted to tell you that I spoke to your parents."

She laughed shortly, imagining just how that conversation had gone. Her parents were still furious with Sam and nothing Mia had said so far had done a thing to cool them down. She knew why, too. Her folks had welcomed Sam into their family. He'd been one of them. Then he'd walked away. From her. From the whole family. And the hurt was as real as the anger.

Maybe she hadn't been able to cool them down because *she* hadn't cooled off, either.

"Well," she said wryly, "I bet that was fun."

He rolled his shoulders, as if he were shrugging off a heavy weight. "Yeah, it was a party." He scowled, then said, "Look, I talked to them because I wanted to give them a heads-up about the storm we might run into tonight."

She blinked at him. Mia had been through storms at sea before and it was never fun. And having a storm so early on the cruise was harder still, because the passengers weren't even accustomed to being on the ship yet—let alone having to deal with high waves and seasickness. "Really? Second night at sea and a storm?"

"Yeah, I know." The wind ruffled his hair and he pushed it off his forehead impatiently, only to have it tossed there again. "We might miss it, but the way this day's going, I think we'll hit it dead-on."

He stared into the distance as if searching for its arrival on the horizon.

"Are you worried?" Mia knew that was a pointless question. Even if he were worried, he'd never admit it. Sam was a man who always projected an aura of calm command.

"No," he said, quickly. "And if it looks like a sure thing, we'll give the other passengers fair warning. But I wanted to tell you and your folks first."

"I appreciate that." She looked up into his eyes and told herself that the coolness reflected there didn't bother her a bit. That was a lie, of course. But then, she was lying to herself about Sam a lot these days. "Now, I'm going to go talk to Maya and Joe, tell them about the storm, so they're prepared just in case."

"That's fine. Just don't tell anyone else," Sam said. "Not yet."

"I won't," she said. "After I talk to my sister, I'm taking Charlie and Chris to the pool. I told them I'd swim with them this afternoon, so their mom and dad can have some time alone."

"Right." He nodded. "They probably need the break from the kids."

Mia cocked her head to one side. "You know, they actually like their children. Most people do."

"Not all," he muttered darkly. His eyes instantly shuttered and Mia recognized the look. Sam was shutting her out of his past, out of whatever it was that had made him so determined to go through his life alone.

She had tried for nearly a year to get past the walls he'd built around himself and hadn't succeeded. Maybe if she had, none of this would be happening. Regret and hurt rose up inside her and Mia had to choke it down.

He stepped aside so she could move past him, then he caught her upper arm and held her in place. "Mia..."

One touch and she was on fire. Mia really resented that he had that power over her. She looked from his hand to his eyes and when he immediately released her, she was sorry for that too. The silky burn of his fingers on her skin remained though, as if to taunt her.

"Was there something else, Sam?"

He looked as though he wanted to say more, but a moment later, he clamped his lips together and shook his head. "No. It's nothing."

Mia's breath caught in her throat and her heartbeat hammered. Standing this close to him was unnerving. She wondered idly if it would always be that way. Would she, in thirty years, run into Sam somewhere, shake his hand and instantly dissolve into a needy puddle?

That thought brought a sting of tears she didn't want to shed. Thirty years without Sam? When she'd been without him for only a few months and already his loss was tearing her apart? How would she ever go the rest of her life without seeing him? Being with him?

By building the kind of life you want, she reminded herself.

And that started in January. All she had to do was get him to sign the papers, survive the rest of this cruise and then she'd be free and clear to begin the journey she'd mapped out for herself.

"Well then. Like I said," Mia whispered, "thanks for the warning about the storm." She left quickly, because if she didn't, she might not leave his side at all.

And where would that get her?

* * *

Of course they hit the storm.

Alone, Sam told himself he should have proposed his 'deal' to Mia when he'd talked to her last. He'd thought about it, but the timing had felt…off. And now, that deal had to be put on the backburner.

"Have to give Kira a raise," Sam muttered. "She called it right down to the hour."

At seven, the first of the heavy waves began to push at the ship, as if trying to turn it around. But the Captain was experienced and one of the best in the world—Sam knew this because he and his brother Michael only hired the best. The ship pushed on and the sea fought them for every mile.

The sky shattered with crashes of thunder and splinters of lightning, illuminating the waves and the empty decks of the ship. The crew were hustling, checking on the passengers, and helping to keep everyone calm, by singing Christmas carols in the dining hall. The youth counselors were keeping the kids busy with games and crafts. For those passengers who'd elected to stay in their suites, their bedroom stewards were doing all they could to help.

Sam spent most of the early evening up on the bridge, where he could watch his employees defy the storm as the ship punched right through the middle of it. By midnight, the waves were a little higher, the decks a little emptier and Sam was tired of being shut up on the computerized bridge that looked futuristic enough to be a spaceship.

Braving the howling wind and the cold sea spray jetting up when wave met hull, Sam stalked the decks, doing his own wellness check. Walking wasn't easy and more than once, he had to make a grab for the railing. But he'd grown up around ships, so he was more than prepared to deal. He didn't run into another soul until he came around the corner on Deck Two, where ordinarily, lines of chaise lounges were set out, tempting passengers to stretch out and enjoy being waited on while they took in a spectacular view.

Now though, the lounges had been folded up and stowed away for safety. It was like a ghost ship—there was only the storm and Sam.

Then he saw her.

His heart leaped. His body burned and he knew that the backburner thing was done. Just one look at her and Sam was in a tangle of need and emotions that both confused and aroused him.

Mia was at the rail. Her hair was a twisted tangle in the wind and she wore jeans, sneakers and a windbreaker that probably wasn't doing much good.

Irritated that she was out by herself in a storm, all he could think was, she might be swept overboard and no one would know it until it was far too late to save her. That thought and the resulting images that appeared in his mind made his blood run cold. With the thought of losing her at the forefront of his mind, Sam stalked to her side and grabbed her arm.

Mia jumped, startled. "Damn it, Sam! You scared the crap out of me!"

"Good," he retorted. "Then we're even. Hell, when I saw you standing out here it damn near stopped my heart. What are you doing out here in this storm?"

"I like it," she said, then pulled her arm from his grasp and turned her back on him as if expecting him to turn around and leave her there alone.

Not going to happen.

He grabbed her again. Hell, the wind was strong enough to pick her up and toss her over the railing. "If you went overboard in this storm, no one would even notice until it was too late to save you."

"I'm not a complete idiot, Sam," she said, not bothering to turn her head to look at him. "I'm not going to fall overboard."

"Yeah, nobody *plans* to fall."

"Honestly," she snapped, finally looking up at him and tugging her arm free again. "I'm not your responsibility. Don't you have something more important to do?"

"Not at the moment," he said, glancing around the empty deck. Close to midnight, the night was quiet but for the thunderous slap of waves against the hull and the now distant growl of thunder. Deck lights threw puddles of lamplight into the darkness, illuminating the deck enough that any late-night wanderer would be safe. When they weren't in a storm.

"I couldn't stay in our suite any longer." She raised her voice to be heard over the cacophony going on around them. "You know I love a storm. At least you should know it."

"I do," he said. And memories crowded his mind. Any time a storm blew in off the ocean, Mia would head out to the balcony off the condo living room to watch it. Most women he'd known worried about their hair, their makeup, but Mia walked into the rain and the wind and never cared what she looked like. Which only made her more beautiful.

And he remembered a night like this one when they were on a cruise to Bermuda. They'd stayed on their private deck and let the storm howl around them like a living thing. They'd laughed like fools as the sea spray and rain soaked them and then the laughter had ended when they made love right there on the rain-slicked private deck.

His body twisted tight and hard and he nearly groaned at the ache that settled on him. That night, Mia had said that the storm was magic—but Sam had always believed that *she* was the magic. Letting her go had been the hardest thing he'd ever done. But if he'd known, even then, that staying with her would have dimmed that magic and he couldn't take the thought of that. He didn't know how to be what she wanted him to be. So for her sake, he'd let her go.

"It's still dangerous, Mia."

"I'll risk it, Sam."

Hardheaded woman. Why did he like that so much? "You should head back to your suite."

"Are you?"

"No, but it's my ship. I want to check a few things."

"Isn't that your crew's job?"

There was an old argument. She'd always believed that he should delegate more. "They're busy. Why are you out here, anyway?"

"I told you, I like storms." When he only stared at her, she blew out a breath, curled her fingers around the top rail and said, "Well, the boys got seasick—though I think it had more to do with the gallons of hot chocolate they had after dinner than the rocking of the ship. That was an ugly hour or so." She grimaced. "Anyway, Maya was cleaning up and then she got sick. Between the ship rocking and the boys—well, another ugly hour. Joe put the boys in my bedroom so Maya could rest and I moved out to the couch to sleep."

"You're going to sleep on the couch?" The sofas were nice, top grade, but sleeping on one wasn't the best idea.

She shrugged. "It's not that bad. So far. Ask me at the end of the cruise. Anyway, I couldn't sleep with all the moaning going on, so I came out here to be *alone.*"

He ignored that not-too-subtle hint, because Sam wasn't about to leave her alone on deck in a storm. "I can have maintenance go to their suite and clean things up."

She tipped her head to one side and looked at him. "Thanks. But not necessary. Our Bed Steward, Robert, helped Joe and I clean things up and most of the misery was over before I left…"

Sam made a mental note to give Robert a bonus. It sounded like he'd earned it. "You don't have to sleep on the couch, Mia."

"Well, it's better than the floor," she said on a half laugh. "And it's not the first time I've slept on a couch."

"No." He took her arm and turned her to face him. The wind buffeted them and sea spray soaked the air from the incessant crashing of the waves against the hull. Her long red hair was tangled and wet. Droplets of water clung to her cheeks and her green eyes were like a forest at twilight in the shadows.

Sam didn't want to feel this need for Mia clawing at his insides. But he didn't know how to make it stop—and even if he could, Sam knew deep in his soul, that he would miss it if it ever ended. What he felt for Mia was unlike anything he'd ever known before and maybe, he thought, that's part of why he'd had to walk away.

It seemed though, that desire for Mia was simply inevitable. She'd had this effect on him from the first moment he'd met her. Nothing had changed. Leaving her hadn't done it. A divorce wouldn't do it. Mia was his wife. Mia was the woman he wanted.

The one he couldn't have once this cruise was over.

His 'plan' rolled through his mind and he smiled to himself. The situation Mia found herself in right now, could feed directly into that plan of his. Now, his idea didn't only benefit him—but her, too.

"You don't have to sleep on a couch, Mia—"

"Well," she said, "I'm not staying in my parents' suite. What if they get frisky? I can't hear that."

"Yeah, I don't want to think about that either," he said. "And I have a solution. You can stay in my suite."

The ship rose up on a wave, then slapped down, making her stagger forward. She slapped both palms on his chest to steady herself. Sam's heartbeat jumped into overdrive.

As if she knew what he was feeling, she shook her head and said, "Oh, no. That is so not a good idea."

"What's the matter?" he asked, a smile curving his mouth. "Don't trust yourself around me?"

"Hah!" She grinned and shook her head. "You would think that, but no."

He didn't believe her. Even over the roar of the storm, he could hear her short, sharp breaths. "Then what's the problem?"

"We're divorced, Sam."

"Not yet."

"Not officially," she amended, shaking her head. "But still."

"It's a two-bedroom suite," Sam reminded her, his voice compelling. "You'd have your own room." *However briefly.*

As if she'd heard his thoughts, she snorted. "And how long would that last?"

"As long as we need it to."

"So," she said, "ten seconds?"

He grinned. "I think it's a great idea."

"Of course you do," she countered, shoving her wet hair off her face.

"Think about it." Sam kept his gaze fixed on hers and he could see, even in the dim light, that in spite of her arguments, she was tempted.

Damn, he'd missed this. Just talking to her. Standing so close to her that he could see her pulse pounding. Looking into green eyes that danced with magic or flashed with fire. He hated that he still missed her. Hated knowing that he probably always would.

He leaned one hip against the railing. Below him, the ocean churned, crashing against the boat. "If you were staying in my suite, Maya and Joe would have a room to themselves…"

"Yes, but—"

"Maya could probably use the break…"

She laughed. "Now you want to do Maya a favor?"

He shrugged. "I'm a great human being."

"Sure." Shaking her head, she looked out to the sea again, so Sam couldn't read her eyes. But he heard the indecision in her voice when she said, "Us sharing a suite would just create more problems, Sam."

"How? Like you said, we're already divorced. What else could go wrong?"

She looked at him. "You know exactly what."

"So again. Don't trust yourself?"

"It's not me I don't trust."

He slapped one hand to his chest and feigned innocence. "Hey, I'm a boy scout."

"Not how I remember it," she muttered.

Sam grinned. He knew how to manage a negotiation and the first step was always, don't show how much you want something. So he'd back off. For now. Let her think about his offer for a couple of days. Always allow the target to think they were in charge. Even when in reality it was Sam's game.

"Think about it, Mia. A room to yourself. Gotta be better than the couch in Maya's suite…"

Shaking her head, she stepped back and looked up at him. "You're doing this on purpose."

"Damn straight."

"Well, that's honest at least."

"It's a new thing I'm trying." He ran his fingertips down the length of her arm.

She shivered and said, "You're staring at me."

"Yeah," he said, moving in closer.

"You're going to kiss me." Her tongue swept her bottom lip and sent a shot of fire racing through him.

"Yeah," Sam said. "You have a problem with that?"

"No." She shook her head slowly for confirmation and added, "I should, but I really don't."

"Good to know." He took her face between his palms, let his gaze slide over her features, painting new memories in his mind. The curve of her cheek, the sigh of her breath, the dip in her top lip that made him want to bite it.

Slowly, so slowly it ached inside him, Sam lowered his head and slanted his mouth over hers. That first taste of her filled his head, his body. She swayed against him and Sam held onto her as if it meant his life. And maybe it did. Because kissing her, feeling her kiss him back, made his heart jolt in his chest as if he were being electrocuted. Every cell in his body sparked into life and hunger for her grew.

Mia wrapped her arms around his waist and he threaded his fingers through her hair, holding her head still. His tongue danced with hers, their breaths mingled, becoming one, then sliding apart again, separate but joined, apart but together.

Seconds ticked into minutes that flew past and at the same time seemed to last forever. And when he finally lifted his head to look down at her, the wind died, the thunder stopped and it felt as if the world was holding its breath while a different storm raged between them.

"This is crazy, Sam," she whispered.

"I don't care," he admitted.

Six

Mia didn't care, either.

Crazy or not, she wanted Sam so badly, it was all she could think about. All she could see. Her hand in his, she held on as he practically ran to the stairs leading up to his suite.

The ship rose and fell with the still roiling waves and Mia hardly noticed.

At the top of the stairs, Sam stopped and took the card key from his shirt pocket. Mia shifted from foot to foot—edgy, needy and well beyond trying to hide what she was feeling.

"Hurry, hurry…"

He shot her a fast look, grinned and quickly slid the key card in and out. The door clicked open and he stepped inside, pulling her in behind him. The room was dark, with only the palest of light streaming through the wall of windows, displaying the stormy ocean beyond the safety of the ship.

She didn't care. She didn't need light. She needed *him*.

"Now, Sam," she whispered, *"now."*

"You got that right," he muttered and yanked her into his arms. Burying his face in the curve of her neck, he kissed her throat, tasted the pounding pulse point there and Mia let her head fall back on a sigh of pleasure.

It had been so long. Too long since she'd felt his hands and mouth on her.

He lifted his head long enough to claim her mouth with his and when their tongues tangled together, Mia was lost. She met him, stroke for stroke, as he walked her backward until her back slammed against the closed door. He broke their kiss as his hands moved up and down her body, cupping her breasts, sliding down to cover her core until Mia writhed against him, arching into his touch.

It wasn't enough.

"Damn it," she whispered, "we weren't supposed to do this."

"Baby," he countered with a half smile, "we were *born* to do this."

Hard to argue.

She unbuttoned his shirt and slid her palms across the broad chest she remembered so well. He hissed in a breath and she smiled to herself, loving that he was as affected as she was. He was beautiful. Muscled, tanned, and so strong, he took her breath away.

"That's it," he muttered, lifting his head to look into her eyes. "Clothes off."

"Oh yeah." She pushed at his shirt, dragging it off his shoulders and he did the same for her, tearing off her windbreaker and then the shirt she wore beneath it. Then his clever hands unhooked the front closure of her bra and a heartbeat later, his palms were covering her breasts. She hissed in a breath and let it slide from her lungs. "Sam..."

His thumbs and forefingers tweaked and pulled at her nipples until Mia whimpered and bit down on her bottom lip to keep from moaning. "That feels so good," she said brokenly.

"Tastes even better," he assured her and bent his head to pull one erect nipple into his mouth. His lips and tongue and teeth pulled at that sensitive bud and Mia was helpless against the onslaught of sensation.

She held his head to her with one hand when he suckled her and she felt that pull deep into her center. Mia licked her lips, watched him sucking her nipple and whispered, "You're killing me."

"No," he murmured against her skin, then lifted his head again to look at her. "I want you alive and screaming my name."

"Good chance of that," she admitted and swallowed hard as one of his hands dropped to the unbuttoned waistband of her jeans and shoved them and her black panties down. Instantly, she stepped out of them, kicked her jeans and panties aside and gave him free rein over her body. His palm covered her heat, his thumb rubbing, rubbing over that tiny bud of coiled need until she groaned aloud and swiveled her hips against his hand.

While he stroked her into mindlessness, she quickly undid Sam's pants, then freed him, curling her fingers around the hard, thick length of him. Sam growled and she smiled to herself, loving the power she had over this strong man. She stroked him, rubbed the tip of him and listened to the harsh, fast breaths that shot from his lungs.

Mia trembled from the need coursing through her. Hearing his response to her, seeing it reflected in his eyes, fed the desire consuming her. And every time he touched her, that pounding drive inside hammered harder, faster.

He dropped both hands to her butt and lifted her off her feet. A rush of fresh excitement slammed through her as she wrapped her legs around his hips and felt his erection brush against her core.

"We're not going to make it to the bedroom this time," Sam murmured.

"Not even close," she agreed and gasped when he pushed himself inside her.

This was what she'd needed. What she'd missed so desperately for the last few months. The way Sam filled her. The way their bodies fit together—as if they were each the missing part of the other.

Mia took a breath and held it, savoring the feel of Sam buried so deeply within her. It was, as it always had been, *magic*. Then he moved and she moaned, letting him hear what he was doing to her. The amazing friction of bodies sliding together. His fingers curled into her butt hard enough to leave imprints on her skin. His breath filling her lungs as he kissed her again, driving his tongue into her mouth, claiming everything she was, silently demanding she hold nothing back. And she didn't. Mouths fused, they tormented each other with the tangle of tongues, the rasping breaths that slid from one to the other of them.

Her hands moved over his back, her nails dragging across his skin and he shuddered as a groan rolled from his throat. His hips rocked hard against her, pushing his erection deep inside. She wiggled against him, wanting more of him. "Harder, Sam. Harder."

"Hold on, honey," he said and quickly set a rhythm that she fought to match.

Desperation fueled his moves and her reaction. There was so much here, so much she'd missed. This was the danger with Sam. That she'd never felt like this with any other man. He was the only one who could make her experience the physical and emotional at the same time.

Again and again, he rocked in and out of her body, pushing her higher than she'd ever been before. Her heels were locked at the small of his back and she pulled him closer, silently demanding more of him.

The low tingle of expectation erupted at her core and Mia chased it, knowing what was waiting for her. She wanted it. Wanted him. He kept her racing toward completion, not giving her a chance to think, hardly allowing her time to breathe. And she didn't care. Who needed to breathe when there was so much more?

His fingers dug into her butt and she squirmed against him. "Sam... Sam..."

"Come on baby, go over," he whispered, staring into her eyes as he claimed her over and over. "Let me watch you. Let me see your eyes."

She wanted him to see what he did to her. Wanted him to know what she was feeling. Mia met his gaze, and held nothing from him. For this moment, all that mattered was Sam and what he was doing to her. She read her own need in his eyes and that was all she needed to finally rush toward the cliff's edge and eagerly jump over.

Mia screamed his name and held onto him tightly as her body exploded from the inside out. Wave after wave of pleasure rocked her, taking her beyond what she thought she could stand, forcing her to feel more and more.

She clung to him, the only stable point in a suddenly upside-down universe. Mia had missed him so much. Missed these moments. The touch of his hand, the warmth of his mouth and the incredible explosions of sheer pleasure that they shared.

Moments, hours, *years* later, Sam finally let go, gave himself up to the same release she'd just experienced, and Mia tightened her grip on him. Holding him to her, loving the way his body bucked and how his eyes went dark, nothing there but the glint of passion.

He called out her name as she held him and locked together, they slid down the other side of need.

When his head cleared, Sam looked into Mia's eyes and gave her a smile. Their bodies were still joined together, and the hum of release was still swimming through his veins. Being with Mia again smoothed out every jagged edge inside him. Sam felt as if after months of being stranded in the icy cold, he'd somehow found his way to a fire that warmed every inch of his body and soul.

And need erupted inside him again. He knew he'd never have enough of her. Be close enough to her.

His hands cupped her behind and his dick jumped to life inside her. "That was…"

Mia took a deep breath. "Yeah, it really was."

"But I'm not done," he admitted, leaning toward her to kiss her once, twice. He wanted more of that fire. The welcoming heat.

When he pulled his head back, she licked her lips, as if savoring the taste of him. And again, his dick reacted.

"I should go," Mia said softly and he felt a sharp stab of disappointment. That lasted only a moment though, before she said, "But I'm not going to. Because I'm not done, either."

"Thank God," Sam murmured and tightened his grip on her, easing her away from the wall.

She laughed and the shuddering of her body sent jolts of new pleasure through his. "I can walk, Sam."

"Yeah, but I like you just where you are."

"Hard to argue," she said as he headed across the darkened room to the master suite. Wiggling against him, she moaned softly at the resulting buzz of sensation.

"You keep that up, we're not going to make it to the bedroom this time, either," he warned.

"Right." She nodded solemnly, then grinned. "So hurry up."

"Yes, ma'am."

Sam had always liked that about Mia. She had no problem letting him know how much she enjoyed sex. How willing she was to try anything.

Instantly, his memories filled with images of her in his bed, against a wall, on the floor, on his kitchen's granite countertops, laid out like a goddess waiting to be adored. And he'd done his best. That night stood out in his mind and had haunted him ever since they'd split up.

It hadn't lasted. He'd lost her. Lost everything because as amazing as the sex was between them, it hadn't been enough to keep them together. But

Get Up To 4 Free Books!

Dear Reader,

IT'S A FACT: if you answer 4 quick questions, we'll send you 4 FREE REWARDS from each series you try!

Try **Harlequin® Desire** books featuring the worlds of the American elite with juicy plot twists, delicious sensuality and intriguing scandal.

Try **Harlequin Presents®** Larger-Print books featuring the glamourous lives of royals and billionaires in a world of exotic locations, where passion knows no bounds.

Or TRY BOTH!

I'm not kidding you. As a leading publisher of women's fiction, we value your opinions... and your time. That's why we are prepared to reward you handsomely for completing our mini-survey. In fact, we have 4 Free Rewards for you, including 2 free books and 2 free gifts from each series you try!

Thank you for participating in our survey,

Pam Powers

www.ReaderService.com

To get your 4 FREE REWARDS:

Complete the survey below and return the insert today to receive up to 4 FREE BOOKS and FREE GIFTS guaranteed!

"4 for 4" MINI-SURVEY

1 Is reading one of your favorite hobbies?
☐ YES   ☐ NO

2 Do you prefer to read instead of watch TV?
☐ YES   ☐ NO

3 Do you read newspapers and magazines?
☐ YES   ☐ NO

4 Do you enjoy trying new book series with FREE BOOKS?
☐ YES   ☐ NO

Please send me my Free Rewards, consisting of **2 Free Books from each series I select** and **Free Mystery Gifts**. I understand that I am under no obligation to buy anything, as explained on the back of this card.

❑ **Harlequin Desire®** (225/326 HDL GQ3X)
❑ **Harlequin Presents® Larger-Print** (176/376 HDL GQ3X)
❑ **Try Both** (225/326 & 176/376 HDL GQ4A)

FIRST NAME   LAST NAME

ADDRESS

APT.#   CITY

STATE/PROV.   ZIP/POSTAL CODE

EMAIL ❑   Please check this box if you would like to receive newsletters and promotional emails from Harlequin Enterprises ULC and its affiliates. You can unsubscribe anytime.

BUSINESS REPLY MAIL
FIRST-CLASS MAIL   PERMIT NO. 717   BUFFALO, NY

POSTAGE WILL BE PAID BY ADDRESSEE

HARLEQUIN READER SERVICE
PO BOX 1341
BUFFALO NY 14240-8571

NO POSTAGE
NECESSARY
IF MAILED
IN THE
UNITED STATES

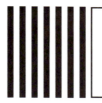

this time with her was something different. Impermanent. Perfect. And he wasn't about to question it.

Now he had her to himself again and he didn't want to waste a second of it. Sam pushed through the open door to his bedroom, stalked across the floor and then laid her down on the king-sized mattress. They were still joined and he didn't want to break that bond, but he did anyway. It almost killed him to pull free of her body and hearing her groan of disappointment didn't help any.

"Don't," she whispered, lifting her hips, letting him see her need. "Be inside me, Sam. I need you inside me."

"I need that too, Mia," he assured her, then went up on his knees and leaned over her.

He dropped his head to her breasts and took first one then the other of her hard, dark pink nipples into his mouth. He loved the taste of her. Always had. And her scent filled his head, fogging his brain as he inhaled her deeper, making that scent a part of him.

Mia held his head to her breast and arched her back, moving into him and when he suckled her, she gasped. His dick aching, his blood pumping, he forced himself to slow down. To appreciate everything about her that he'd missed.

Her skin was so soft, her body so curvy and lean at the same time. And so willing. So eager.

He trailed his mouth down her rib cage, across that flat abdomen of hers and down to her center.

"Sam?"

"I'm hungry for you, Mia," he said, catching her gaze with his. He paused briefly to watch her eyes flash and then he knelt between her legs, held her open for him and covered her with his mouth.

"Sam!" Her shout echoed in the room and reverberated in his mind, his soul.

He ran his tongue over her center, licking, nibbling. Her legs trembled in his hands, but she lifted her hips blindly, helplessly, trying to feel more. He sucked at the nub of sensation crowning her core and he felt her body shake. Her breath quickened with every stroke of his tongue.

Sam listened to her whimpers, moans, pleas for release and those soft sounds fed the fires inside him. He pushed two fingers into her depths while his mouth worked that tiny nub of passion until she was a breath away from completion.

Then he stopped.

"What? What?" Her eyes sprang open and she stared at him. "You can't stop now. What are you doing to me, Sam?"

"Enjoying you, Mia," he said, then took hold of her hips and with one quick move, flipped her over onto her stomach.

"Oh." She threw her hair back out of her eyes and looked at him over her left shoulder. A tiny smile tugged at one corner of her mouth and then she licked her lips again. Slowly, slowly, she went up on her knees and Sam smoothed his palms over her behind.

"That's my girl," he murmured and edged off the

mattress, pulling her along with him. When he was standing behind her, he held onto her hips and drove himself inside her.

Mia tipped her head back, pushed hard against him and moved in time with the rhythm he set. Back in her heat, Sam gave himself over to the moment. Rocking into her body again and again, he took them both as high as they'd ever been and then went further.

"Sam! Sam!" Mia's body shattered quickly, because she had been so close when he'd changed things up. She trembled and cried out again and now, when he was so close to joining her, he changed again.

He pulled free of her, flipped her onto her back and lay down on top of her. Sliding into her once more, he stared into her eyes, shadowed, passion-glazed, and let himself take that long, last leap into the kind of passion pool he'd only found with Mia.

Exhausted, energized, Mia lay on Sam's big bed and looked over at the wall of windows. She knew the glass had been treated, so that no one could see *into* the suite. Which made it easy to feel decadent, naked with her lover—her husband—and displayed to a world who couldn't know what was going on behind the glass.

She hadn't meant for this to happen, but maybe it was always going to end here. In bed. She and Sam had always had an extremely physical relationship.

When everything else in their marriage had begun to dissolve, the sex had never lost its magic.

Turning her head on the pillow to look at the man sprawled beside her, Mia had to smile. Even in sleep, he was contained, pulled into himself. There was no leg tossed over hers. No arm reaching out for her. And that broke her heart a little, as it always had. She wished she knew why Sam spent most of his time trying to keep her at a distance. But his brother Michael had refused to talk, insisting it was Sam's story to tell.

She agreed. The only problem was, Sam wouldn't tell it. And until she knew what she was fighting against, how could she win? She couldn't. Which was why Mia had finally admitted defeat and accepted that their marriage was over. Outside, the storm had passed and moonlight was fading into the first hint of the coming sunrise. That thought propelled her off the mattress, which instantly brought Sam awake.

"Where you going?"

She stood up and scooped her hair back from her face. "I have to get back to the couch in Maya's suite."

He went up on one elbow. "Why? Just stay here."

Mia laughed and shook her head. "I don't think so. Maya doesn't need to know what happened here."

That was all she needed. Wasn't this exactly what her twin had been warning against? She really didn't want to hear Maya on the subject because Mia was already giving herself a stern, internal talking-to.

"Ashamed?" he asked.

"No."

The one-word answer encompassed everything she was feeling. She wasn't embarrassed or ashamed or whatever else he might accuse her of being. Heck, she couldn't even regret this because she hadn't felt this good in months. Her body was loose and limber and her mind was filled with new memories that would have to last her a lifetime. Because this time with him hadn't changed anything.

"Great," he said. "Then stay."

The man was almost impossible to argue with because generally, he could *not* be budged from his point of view. That's the way it had been throughout their marriage. Sam did what he wanted when he wanted. He'd never learned to bend. To give a little.

And she needed more than that.

"I can't." She turned then and walked naked out of the bedroom.

Outside the sky was lightening and she knew that soon, the boys would be awake and Maya only moments later. Mia really had to hurry.

Of course, Sam followed her into the living room, as naked as she and so tempting, she couldn't trust herself to look at him for long.

She passed the dining table and noticed the envelope containing their divorce papers. "Did you sign the papers?"

"Not yet," he said from right behind her.

Mia grabbed her jeans and panties from the floor.

Stuffing her torn underwear into one of the pockets, she pulled the still damp denim on and shivered with the cold. "What's the problem?"

"What's the rush?" he countered.

Sighing, Mia bent over to pick up her bra and shirt. Thankfully, Sam hadn't ripped her bra as casually as he had her panties. She pulled on the black lace bra and hooked it. "I have plans," she said. "Starting in January. I need you to sign those papers."

"What plans?" he asked, crossing his arms over his chest. His feet were braced apart and he stood there staring at her like an ancient god.

Her mouth went dry, but still, she managed to say, "None of your business."

"It is if you want me to sign."

Mia paused to slip on her cold, damp blouse. "Blackmail? Really?"

"Oh, I haven't given you the blackmail offer yet."

Staring at him, she said, "You're serious."

"Damn serious." He walked toward her and Mia backed up. A naked Sam was far too dangerous. "You want those papers signed. I want more time with you in my bed. And I want to know your big secret plans."

"Sam."

Shaking his head, he said, "Think about it. You move into my suite for the duration of the cruise. When we're back in Long Beach, I sign the papers and we're done."

Her heart was pounding and her mind whirling. She should have expected this. Hadn't he been trying to get her into his suite all along? Of course the businessman in him would use whatever leverage he had to get the outcome he wanted.

"So you're blackmailing me into having sex with you to get what I want."

"To get what we *both* want," he corrected.

She could fight him on this, but what would be the point? She'd proven only moments ago how much she wanted him, too. They had a little less than two weeks on this cruise together. Was she going to pretend that sex wouldn't happen between them again? Would she pretend she wasn't going to spend her nights slipping out of Maya's suite to come up here and be with Sam, then sneak back to that couch in the morning?

Sam walked closer and Mia knew she should move back, but she didn't. It was a little late to be circumspect. Barn door open. Horse gone.

He stepped up to her and slid his hands beneath the open edges of her shirt, skimming his fingertips across her skin until she sighed with resignation. There was simply no denying this. She wanted Sam. Always would.

So if the next two weeks was all she'd have of him, then she could be called the world's first willing blackmail victim.

"What do you say, Mia?" Sam bent his head to the column of her throat and kissed his way up to her mouth. By the time he got there, she was weak-kneed and helpless to say anything but what he wanted to hear.

"I say it's a deal." When he lifted his head, she met his gaze and tried to read everything written in those depths she had once thought she knew so well. But he was a master at negotiations and all he allowed her to see was his satisfaction.

"So you'll move in here tonight."

It wasn't a question. "Yes," she said, and batted his hands away so she could button up her shirt. Looking around, she spotted her shoes where she'd kicked them off a lifetime ago.

She walked over, stepped into the slip-on sneakers then looked at Sam. He was exactly what Maya had always called him. *Mia's Kryptonite.* Even now, all she wanted to do was step into his arms and let him carry her back to the bedroom.

"And you'll sign the divorce papers." Also not a question.

His eyes flashed, but he nodded. "I will."

"Okay then. I'll see you later." While she still could, she opened the door, slipped outside and hurried back to Maya's suite. And on the way, she tried to come up with the words she would use to tell her family about what she was doing.

By the following afternoon, it was as if the storm had never happened.

Passengers were out enjoying the pool area, the

spas and the shopping pavilions on the Sun Deck. At one end of the Sun Deck, the pool, hot tubs and the swim-up bar were busy. But at the opposite end, passengers were crowded around the five food stations, offering everything from sushi to sandwiches to stuffed Belgian waffles. And the shops were just as crowded. It looked to Sam as though everyone on board ship was determined to celebrate the end of the storm and the return of smooth sailing.

He walked the perimeters of the crowd, because he'd learned long ago that the best way to learn what people thought of your business was to interact with them. Watch them with the employees, and make mental notes of where to improve.

It was a party atmosphere, and even Sam couldn't help smiling at the small group of children playing by one of the Christmas trees set up on the promenade. When he realized what he was doing, his smile slipped away. Kids? Really? What the hell was that?

Were Mia and her family getting to him?

He shook his head and kept walking, skirting the edges of the crowd, making more mental notes on the waiters, the stewards, the chefs working the food stalls. Nothing escaped Sam's attention. Not the smallest detail. Though the traffic flow through this section seemed to be working well enough, Sam realized that putting more distance between the food stalls themselves would allow the passengers to get a better idea of what was being offered.

Waiters worked the crowd, delivering meals and

drinks and the shops on this level were packed with customers. He appreciated how well the Christmas-themed cruise seemed to be working. The passenger list was mostly families and he told himself that it might be time to consider adding a few family cruises to their yearly lineup.

By banning kids from most of their voyages, they were cheating themselves out of hundreds of thousands of potential passengers. His brother Michael had made that same argument many times, but Sam had never been interested. Their father had started the adults-only cruises and Sam had never seen the point in changing something that was clearly working.

But now, he had to admit that family cruises could be very successful for the Buchanans. He'd have to talk to Mike about it. And even as he told himself that, Sam realized that he never would have considered making the change before this trip and a part of him wondered why he was doing it now.

He remembered the looks on the faces of his nephews—the excitement. The...well, the *joy* and multiplied it by the number of kids onboard. Maybe it was because this was a Christmas cruise and the kids would be excited by the holiday no matter where they were, but Sam had the feeling that being onboard a ship sparked the same kind of excitement in most of them.

"Sam!" He stopped, looked around until he spotted Joe Rossi, sitting at a table with their father-in-law.

Joe waved one hand and said, "Come sit down for a minute."

Sam hesitated, trying, he could admit to himself, to find a way out. But there wasn't one. And damned if he'd go into hiding on his own damn ship. He could handle a quick conversation for God's sake. He threaded his way past the crowded tables and stopped beside Joe and Henry's. Each man had a beer in front of him and in the center of the table was a huge bowl of nachos, corn chips smothered in cheese, onions, peppers and shredded beef.

"You make it through the storm all right?" he asked, looking from one man to the other.

"It was rough for a while," Joe admitted with a laugh. "But things are looking up now." He pulled out a chair. "Sit down, Sam."

He glanced at Henry and the older man nodded. With no way out of spending a little time with his in-laws, Sam took a seat and signaled a passing waiter for a beer. He had the feeling he was going to need one.

"Mia told me the kids and then Maya were sick last night."

Joe's eyebrows arched. "She did, huh? Well, she wasn't lying. But everyone's better today. My A plus mother-in-law has the kids in the craft room making Christmas presents and Maya's relaxing with Mia at the spa."

That explained why he hadn't spotted Mia anywhere on the ship during his walkabout.

"When did you see Mia last night?" Joe asked.

Sam shifted a look to Henry. The older man was pretty cagey and always seemed to know more than he let on. So that led to the question—*what did he know about what had happened last night?*

"During the storm, late last night. I found her at the railing by the pool." Of course, that wasn't where he'd left her, but they didn't need to know that.

Joe winced. "That's probably our fault. Between the kids and then Maya getting sick…"

Henry nodded, never taking his gaze from Sam's. "No, Mia's always loved a good storm. And living in California meant she didn't get to see many."

"She does love the wind and rain," Sam said. He remembered again how Mia would stand out on the balcony of their condo to watch anytime there was a storm. Be a part of it.

Henry leaned forward, picked up his beer and sat back again. "I wanted to talk to you, Sam. Without the women around."

The waiter delivered Sam's beer, then disappeared into the crowd again. Sam lifted it, took a sip, then held onto the icy bottle as he waited for whatever it was his father-in-law was going to say next. He didn't have to wait long.

"I'm listening," Sam said tightly, waiting for the man to come down on him for breaking up with Mia. Or for hooking up with her last night. Or for not signing the damn divorce papers. Whatever it was though, Sam would take it. Out of respect for Mia's father.

He just hoped that Henry didn't somehow know what had happened between him and Mia last night during the storm. And what was going to happen the minute he got her alone again.

"You made a big mistake, Sam."

Well, that caught his attention. Sam didn't make mistakes often, but when he did, he surely didn't need someone else to tell him about them. "I don't think so, Henry."

The older man laughed shortly and shook his head. "That's because you can't see far enough ahead of you yet."

"Henry…" Sam paused, took a sip of beer and used that moment to think of something to say. But Henry beat him to it when he continued.

"Yeah, this is my talk, Sam," he said. "So you just sit there and listen, all right? I want you to know, Emma's still pretty pissed at you."

"Yeah, I caught onto that yesterday," Sam said wryly, remembering how his mother-in-law had talked *about* him as if he didn't really exist.

Henry smirked and shrugged. "She protects our girls with everything she's got. And when one of them gets hurt, then God help whoever caused that pain."

"Yeah," Joe put in. "We've been married eight years and Emma still hasn't forgiven me for standing Maya up one time when we first started dating."

"You're kidding." Sam just stared at him.

"I wish."

"The point is," Henry said, getting both of their attention again, "I want you to know that I get it."

All right, that he hadn't expected to hear. "You do?"

"You're not the first man to have the crap scared out of him by marriage."

Well, that was insulting. If he'd been scared of marriage he wouldn't have married Mia in the first place. He was scared of dropping his own issues onto Mia and corrupting her with them. He'd wanted her—loved her—enough to try, though in spite of the niggling doubts inside him. Hell, a part of him had hoped that she would be his cure. But he hadn't been able to let her get close enough to try. "I don't get scared, Henry. And I sure as hell wasn't scared of Mia."

"Didn't say you were. Said you were scared of marriage."

"And you're wrong again. I just wasn't any good at it." It cost him to admit that.

"Hardly gave yourself long enough to find that out, did you?"

"It was long enough, Henry." Sam set his beer down and looked at the older man. He had never liked explaining himself and didn't want to do it now. But maybe he owed Henry something. "I thought it was better that I leave when I did than wait until we were farther down the road."

"Uh-huh."

There was a smirk on Henry's face that irritated Sam so that he spoke up again quickly. "Better I left when I did. Yeah, she was hurt. But if I'd stayed, it would only have gotten worse."

Joe gave a long, low whistle and Sam frowned at him. What the hell did that mean?

"So you're the hero, is that it?"

His head snapped around to Henry again. "I didn't say that, either."

"Son, I'll tell you right now, you've cheated yourself and Mia out of what you might have made together. I don't believe you've got the first clue about what you're doing here."

Sam had had the same thought many times, but he knew himself. Knew that if he'd stayed with Mia, it would have become a misery and he wanted to save her—and himself—from that kind of pain.

"Maybe not, but it's my decision. Mine and Mia's."

"No, just yours. If it was her call to make, you wouldn't have split up."

"Mia's the one who asked for the divorce, Henry."

"That's true, but I'm guessing she didn't expect you to agree."

"You should ask her how she feels about it now," Sam muttered and took another drink of his beer.

Sex didn't count.

The sex between him and Mia had always been amazing. He'd never been with a woman he could laugh with during sex. Never had a woman touch him the way she did. But that wasn't enough to build a marriage on. It wasn't enough to make up for the fact that Sam had no damn idea how to be in a relationship for the long haul.

"All I'm saying is you should use this cruise to take a hard look at what you gave up," Henry said. "And ask yourself—was it worth it?"

Sam had been asking himself that question for months. And he still didn't have an answer.

"One more thing," Henry said, his voice low and tight. "If, when the cruise is over, you can't see what a treasure my daughter is—then you sign those papers and you let her go."

Seven

While Joe and Maya's dad were having a beer, the kids participated in a Christmas-themed scavenger hunt. Under the supervision of what appeared to be a battalion of crew members, children raced around the boat trying to find all of the objects on their lists.

When that was over, Emma Harper took her grandsons to the Christmas craft room to make presents for their family. Which gave Maya and Mia time to enjoy a spa day. After facials and a mani/pedi, the twins lay stretched out on plush, luxurious chaises waiting for their nails to dry.

"You don't have to stay on the couch," Maya said for what had to be the tenth time that morning. "The boys are feeling better so you can have your room back."

Mia had made it back to the couch before everyone got up and she was grateful for that. But the truth was, Maya and Joe both looked rested after getting a good night's sleep and the boys had a ball in their adjoining room. Sam had been right about that. Joe hadn't complained about anything, but she knew that part of the reason for this trip had been to give him a chance to rest up, too.

Joe and several other firemen from his company had just returned from fighting a fire in Idaho and he could use all the rest he could get.

"Yeah, about that," Mia said. "It's better with you and Joe having your own room. The boys get to laugh and talk to each other half the night."

"Sure," Maya said, pausing for a sip of her pomegranate fizz, "but you deserve more than a couch."

"I agree." She took a breath and added, "So, I've found a room and I'm moving into it when we're finished here." Of course, she knew her twin and was absolutely sure that Maya wouldn't accept that statement at face value. Mia had been dreading this conversation all morning. But the time had come, whether she liked it or not. Besides, this wasn't about Maya or what she thought. Mia was moving in with Sam because she wanted this time with him. It wasn't forever. Heck it wouldn't last longer than this cruise. But God, she needed him so badly, she was willing to put up with the inevitable pain to come just to have him now.

Maya pushed herself up on her elbows and looked at her. "How'd you find a room? The ship is sold out. Did you toss someone overboard?"

"No."

"What's going on with you? You keep getting really quiet, like you used to in school when you were figuring out how to do something without me."

Mia forced a laugh. "You're paranoid."

"No, just hugely pregnant and out of patience. So why don't we cut through everything else and you just tell me what's going on?"

"Okay, fine." Mia swung her legs over the side of the chaise and faced her sister. "I met Sam last night…"

"When?"

"Right after the hot chocolate plague."

Her features screwed up. "Ew. Don't blame you for leaving, even if it was in a storm. And you saw Sam where?"

"Out on the Sun Deck and…"

"And?" Maya's eyes narrowed on her and Mia wondered why she was feeling guilty. For heaven's sake, until they were divorced, she and Sam were married. Why was it bad that she'd had sex with her husband? And why was she leery about telling Maya?

"And we went back to his suite."

"God. You had sex, didn't you?" Maya struggled

to sit up and lost. The mound of her belly kept getting in the way. She held out one hand to her sister and Mia stood up, grabbed that hand and hauled her twin into a sitting position. "My God, I forget what it's like to just sit up whenever the hell you want to," Maya grumbled.

Then louder, she said, "I knew you had a *just had sex* glow and I told myself I had to be wrong because my twin wouldn't be so stupid as to waltz right back into Sam's bed."

"Not stupid."

"Just horny?"

"Maya." Exasperated, Mia sighed heavily. "He's still my husband."

Maya waved that off. "A technicality."

"A fairly important one." Mia sipped at her drink and paced the small, private room. The spa treatment rooms were, of course, luxurious and soothing, with their cream-colored walls dotted with pastoral paintings and thick, pale blue carpet. The furnishings were designed to calm, relax. But, she told herself, it was going to take more than that to cool Maya down.

"Mia, you're supposed to be over him, remember?" Maya stared at her. "We're here so he'll sign the divorce papers and let you start the life you want to have. And you're sleeping with him?"

"Not sleeping," she mused and couldn't quite keep a half smile from curving her mouth.

"No need to brag," her twin snapped. "Has he signed the papers yet?"

"Not yet, but he will."

"And you know this how?"

"He told me he would." She took a sip of her fizz to ease a dry throat. "When we get back to Long Beach, he'll sign."

Maya studied her through narrowed eyes. "Why are you so sure all of a sudden?"

"I just am, Maya. Leave it at that." She really didn't want to confess that she'd been blackmailed into this deal, because even though it had given her the excuse she'd needed to do what she wanted all along, the truth was just too humiliating to admit that she was a willing victim.

"I don't think so."

"How about looking at it like this—if I'm right there with him, I can make sure he signs those papers."

"Sure. You sharing a suite with Sam and you're going to be thinking about business."

"He'll be a captive audience, won't he?"

She wanted her sister on her side because it would make things much easier. But the bottom line was, she'd already made her decision. She didn't like sleeping on the couch. Sharing a suite with her sister and the family was harder than she might have thought. Just the bathroom situation alone was enough to make her go for it.

And she almost laughed at her own ridiculous explanations for what she was doing. The simple truth was, she wanted to be with Sam. They had this cruise together and then they were finished.

She wanted this time with him.

Still…when they were married, Sam was rarely around. He didn't spend time with her—except at night in their bedroom. So wouldn't he find ways to stay busy somewhere on the ship? Probably. But the ship was a lot smaller than the city of Long Beach. He'd have a much harder time avoiding her, especially if she was sharing his room.

"Oh man…" Maya shook her head. "This is what I'm worried about."

"What?"

"You *want* him captive. You still *want* him."

"I didn't say that."

"You didn't have to."

"You're wrong," Mia lied and silently congratulated herself on sounding so convincing. "What I want is the future I'm planning. To get that, I have to deal with Sam."

And that's all she would do. She'd already made arrangements to move her life forward. That began in January and Mia wouldn't let anything stop it.

"Look, this will work out for all of us. You guys get your own room. I don't have to stay on a couch…" She threw up one hand. "Why shouldn't I stay with him? He's got the room. We're still married."

"And Sam's doing this just to be nice?"

"You have a suspicious mind."

"I know. I like it." Maya sighed. "What I don't like is that you're getting drawn back in when you were fighting your way out. I don't want to see you crying for him again, Mia."

She didn't want that either, but she had a feeling there was no way to avoid it. So if she had to pay later for what she wanted today, then she'd pay. She'd missed him too much to deny herself this chance to be with him again, however briefly. He was worth the coming pain. He was worth everything to Mia.

"I love you for that sweetie, I really do. But this is my decision."

Maya nodded grimly. "And your plans for January? Is that still a go?"

"Yes," she said quickly. "This doesn't change that. I still want children. I'm still going to keep my appointment at the sperm bank. But I need Sam's signature on those papers so there's no legal confusion when I do get pregnant."

She didn't want to risk still being married when she was pregnant through a donor. It might bring up custody issues and who knew how many other problems. No, she would stay with Sam until he signed the papers and then she would be free to build the family she'd always wanted. If she had to do that alone, she was ready. She had her extended family to stand with her and though her baby wouldn't have a father, Mia would make sure her child would never doubt how much it was loved.

"Okay, I won't say anything else about it…"

"Thank you."

"But—"

"I knew it," Mia muttered.

"If Sam makes you cry again, I make no promises."

She'd just make sure Maya never saw her cry. "That's so reasonable, I'm not sure who you are now."

Maya laughed, drained her pomegranate fizz, then set the glass down. "Okay, I'm done. Let's go pack your stuff so you can get started on your hormonal journey."

"Maya…"

After that "talk" with Mia's father, Sam had had enough of people. He went back to his suite and busied himself with the blueprints for their new ship. Sipping at coffee he really didn't taste and staring at the intricate details of what would be the Buchanan line's first Clipper ship, he tried to concentrate, but how the hell could he?

Ridiculous. When he and Mia were together, he hadn't had any trouble focusing on his company. All he'd had to do was remind himself that their marriage was doomed and that was enough to keep himself laser focused on business. He'd known that Mia wouldn't be satisfied with a husband who couldn't give her what she needed—real intimacy. And he couldn't bring himself to tear down the walls he'd built around himself. Not even for her. They were too strong. Too implacable. But he hadn't been scared.

"Scared?" He snorted, picked up his coffee cup and took a swallow, only to gag when he discovered it had gone icy cold.

He set the cup down, pushed away from the dining table and the detailed plans he'd been trying to study. Instead he walked to the French doors and stepped out onto his private balcony.

The ocean wind rushed at him as if welcoming a long-lost friend. The scent of the sea and the distant sounds of people having a good time reached him and Sam wondered why the hell he felt so alien on his own damn boat.

He didn't fit in with the passengers. Or with Mia's family. Or hell, even with Mia. And yet she was all he could think about. He didn't much like that and hated admitting it, even to himself. But the truth was there and couldn't be avoided.

Mia's eyes, her smile, her laugh, plagued his memory. The way she moved, the way she sipped at a glass of wine then licked her bottom lip in a slow swipe. The sounds she made when they had sex. The way her hair fell around her shoulders as if it were caressing her.

The last few months without her hadn't been easy, but at least not seeing her had allowed him to tell himself that his memories were cloudy. That he was remembering everything surrounded by some stupid rosy glow.

But being with her again forced him to acknowledge that there was no rosy glow. It was all true.

Every memory. Every haunted dream. And now she was moving in here with him just so he could what? Torture himself further?

"What's the damn point?"

Sex, his brain shouted at him.

And yeah, true. But also true was that being around her now wouldn't change anything. He'd still be a bad bet for marriage and that's what Mia wanted. What she deserved. A family. Husband. Kids. And as bad as he was as a husband, Sam felt sure he'd fail even more spectacularly as a father. Since he didn't allow himself to fail, he wouldn't put himself in a position to do just that…again. Marrying Mia the first time, when he'd known going in that it wouldn't last, had been the exception. He shouldn't have done it. He knew now he couldn't give her what she wanted so why was he going to take this time with her only to cut ties and leave again?

Because he wanted her.

More than his next breath, Sam wanted Mia.

Whatever it cost him.

Whatever it cost them both.

The knock on the door brought him up from his thoughts. He stalked across the living room, threw the door open and stared at Mia. She wore a pale yellow, short-sleeved shirt with a deep neckline and a string of tiny buttons down the front. The shirt was tucked into a pair of cream-colored slacks and her heeled brown sandals displayed toes painted a dark purple.

Her long, reddish-gold hair was a tumble of waves around her face and draped across her shoulders. Her green eyes watched him and, in the sunlight, he noticed the spray of golden freckles across her nose and cheeks.

In her three-inch heels, they were nearly eye to eye and all Sam could think was that he'd always liked that she was tall. Made it so much easier to kiss her.

"Are you just going to look at me?" she asked, tipping her head to one side. "Or are you going to help me carry my stuff inside?"

"I can do both," he assured her and still bent down to grab her suitcase. He stepped back and waved her inside, then followed and closed the door behind them.

Glancing at him, she said, "I thought I'd put my things in the second bedroom."

He'd wondered if she would try to back away from their deal. "You did? Why?"

"Because we're not here to play house, are we?" she asked. "It's sex we're both after, not *real* intimacy, right?"

He set her bag down. "I think we were pretty intimate yesterday." And he couldn't wait to be *intimate* with her again.

"Our bodies, sure," she said, dropping her brown leather bag onto the nearest table. "But that's all."

"Not enough for you?" he asked, even knowing the answer. Of course it wasn't enough. The sex they'd shared when they were together had been amazing, and it hadn't been enough. She'd still wanted out. Just as he'd known she would.

"It shouldn't be enough for anyone," she countered.

"Fine. Stay where you want," he said tightly. Damned if he'd *ask* her to stay in his bedroom. "But no matter where you sleep, our deal stands."

"I won't back out. And you won't back out of signing those papers, either."

"I won't."

"Good, then it's settled."

If it was, it sure as hell didn't feel like it.

She walked to the second bedroom and stepped inside. Sam followed after her, carrying the hot-pink suitcase. He set it down on the queen-sized bed, then folded his arms across his chest and watched her as she moved about the room.

It was smaller than his suite and the bathroom wasn't nearly as impressive, but he guessed she didn't care about any of that. "It suit you?"

She turned toward him, swinging her hair back from her face. "It's fine."

Nodding, he asked, "What did you tell Maya about where you were going?"

"The truth."

Perfect. "Bet she was happy to hear that."

Mia smiled briefly. "Believe it or not, she used to like you. A lot."

Wryly he said, "She hid it well." Why were they so

stiff and polite all of a sudden? What had happened to the woman who'd been completely free and open with him yesterday? Was she rethinking their deal? And if she was, why was she here at all?

"Why are you here?" he asked aloud.

"You know why," she answered. "I need you to sign the divorce papers."

"And…"

She took a deep breath and let it out again slowly. "And, because I want you. I never stopped wanting you."

"I feel the same," he admitted. Then felt as though he should say more. Should make sure she knew that whatever they shared for the next ten days or so, nothing would change the reality between them. "You need to know, Mia, and to remember, that when we get back to Long Beach, everything between us ends. Again."

Mia laughed shortly and shook her head. "Do you think I'm daydreaming about white picket fences, Sam? No. I learned my lesson. You're a very good teacher."

The expression on her face tore at him. Hurt. Anger. Disappointment, before she buried it all beneath a small smile and cool green eyes. He pushed one hand through his hair, then scrubbed the back of his neck as he searched for the words he wanted.

"I didn't set out to hurt you, Mia."

"Imagine if you'd put some effort into it," she quipped and the sting of the words stabbed at him.

"Right. Hell, I knew before we got married that it wouldn't work out. I knew it was pointless."

Pointing her finger at him, Mia said, "And that's the attitude that killed it."

"What's that supposed to mean?" He hadn't killed anything. He'd married her, hadn't he? Even when he knew it would fall apart.

"Oh Sam." She sighed. "That's so pitiful. You knew it wouldn't work out. Don't you get it? That was a self-fulfilling prophecy."

"Seriously?"

"Yes. If you were so sure our marriage would fail, then you didn't have to try to make it work. So when it ended, you could pat yourself on the back and say *See? I was right*."

While she opened her suitcase and unpacked, Sam stood in the doorway, considering. He'd never thought of it like that before and he didn't much care for the idea now, either. Besides, did it matter why their marriage had come apart? The point was that it had and the only thing Sam was interested in was *now*.

Then he scowled again when he realized that not long ago, she'd accused him of thinking only of the now. Her being right about that was more irritating than he wanted to admit. How the hell had they gotten onto this anyway? He didn't need therapy and if he did, he wouldn't go looking for it from his almost ex-wife.

"So why did you ask me to marry you in the first place?" she asked.

"Now you want the answer to that?"

"Better late than never," she quipped. "You said you knew it would fail, but you did it anyway. Why?"

"Because I wanted you."

"Not good enough."

He pushed one hand through his hair. "I wanted…"

"What, Sam? What did you want?"

"To belong, I guess." Sam's mouth snapped shut but it was too late, a bit of the truth had slipped out.

"Oh Sam, you did belong. With me." She shook her head. "And you let me go."

Yeah he had and she had no idea how much that had cost him. Losing Mia had been like ripping his own heart out. And still he'd done it because he'd believed it was better for both of them.

"So the plan is to give me a hard time?"

Her mouth worked and her eyebrows arched. "I don't think I'm in charge of the hard time."

"Funny. But the question stands."

"Oh relax, Sam. I'm not going to torture you or anything. It looks like you're doing a good enough job of that on your own." She carried a toiletry kit into the bathroom and glanced around. "Hmm. Tiny."

"You can use mine," he said.

"Thanks. I might." She came back into the room and looked up at him. "Anyway, you barely listened to me when we were married, so why would you listen now?"

"I listened."

She rolled her eyes and he gritted his teeth. Maybe having her stay with him hadn't been such a great idea after all.

"I thought we'd have dinner on our balcony tonight," he said, changing the subject. "I'll have the chef send up his specialties."

"Oh." She bit her bottom lip.

"Problem?"

Shrugging, she said, "I already ordered an early dinner to be sent up. It should be here any minute, actually."

"Really?" He smiled, feeling better about this whole thing. An intimate dinner, just the two of them, then to bed. Worked for him. "That's great. I'm glad you're comfortable here."

"Oh, absolutely." A knock on the door sounded and Mia patted his arm. "That's dinner."

It was only five, but if she wanted dinner now, Sam would find a way to be hungry. Besides, the earlier they ate, the earlier he could get her into bed, where he most wanted her. He followed her out and saw her open the door to two crew members carrying trays. Whatever she'd ordered, there was plenty of it.

"Oh, thanks, Brian," she said. "Can you guys just put it on the dining room table?"

"Sure thing, Mrs. Buchanan."

Sam moved fast, getting to the table first and sweeping up the ship blueprints he'd been studying earlier. Two covered trays were set down on the polished teak table and then the first steward asked, "Is there anything else we can get you?"

"No," she said, "that's great. Thanks again. Oh, is Steven on his way?"

"Yes, ma'am. And Devon's bringing the rest of the stuff you asked for."

She beamed at him and Sam couldn't blame the kid for flushing bright red. "Terrific."

"What stuff?" Sam asked and Brian slipped out the door to avoid having to answer the boss.

"You'll see," Mia told him.

"Fine." Sam looked at the trays a little warily. "So what's for dinner?"

"That's a surprise, too," Mia said with a grin, then turned to the door at the sound of a kid shouting.

Sam frowned but couldn't look away. As the stewards left, a young woman in a crew uniform approached, holding two kids by the hand. Maya's kids. Sam just barely muffled a groan.

"Aunt Mia, hi!" Charlie pulled free and raced to her.

Mia bent down to hug him, then grabbed Chris close too, as soon as the young woman got him up the stairs. "Hi you guys! Are you ready for your party?"

"Christmas tree?" Chris asked, looking past her into the barren, if luxurious suite.

"Soon, sweetie," she assured him. "Now why don't we go have dinner? It's your favorite. Hot dogs!"

"Yay!" Charlie raced to the table, shouting "Hi Uncle Sam," as he passed.

Both kids raced across the elegant carpet, leaving a trail of sweaters and what looked like bits of snow in their wake.

"Hot dogs?" Sam looked at her as she led Chris to the table, too.

"I thought it would be nice for us to give Maya and Joe and my folks an evening off. We can spend some time with the kids and the adults can go have dinner together." She shrugged and gave him a wide-eyed, innocent smile.

"Uh-huh." He glanced to where Charlie was standing on a hand carved chair, trying to lift one of the tray covers. Sam moved fast. He lifted the heavy cover, then told Charlie to sit down.

"I like ketchup," Chris said, scrambling for a seat himself.

"Mine's mustard, right Aunt Mia?"

"Right, sweetie." Mia moved up to the table and set out plates for both boys and fixed hot dogs for each of them. "Here's some mac and cheese, too. Don't use your fingers, Charlie. Chris, do you want some? And we've got juice boxes here somewhere too." She lifted the other lid, found juice and glasses and ice, along with a plate of chocolate chip cookies for dessert.

Chris reached for a juice and tipped the glass over. A river of what looked like cherry juice ran across the table and over the edge to land on the hand woven rug.

Sam muffled a groan and dropped a stack of napkins on the puddle. He was not set up for small children.

"I need more juice," Chris whined.

"Sure sweetie," Mia cooed and took care of that.

Sam was watching it all as if from a distance. His personal space had been invaded by a horde of barbarians and all he could do was watch.

"Yay! Can we watch a movie about Christmas because we get to decorate a Christmas tree and where is your tree, Uncle Sam?"

Sam's ears were ringing, but he stared at Mia as if he'd never seen her before. He should have suspected something when she'd arrived. She had been too smiley. Too accepting of the whole situation. Of course she'd had something planned.

"Christmas tree?" he asked.

She shrugged and smiled again. "If I'm going to stay here with you, we need to get into the spirit."

"Mia…" He didn't do Christmas and she damn well knew it. What was she up to? Trying to drag him, kicking and screaming, into the holiday? And using the kids to guilt him into agreeing?

"Steve, the cruise host is bringing in one of the trees that wasn't set up." She paused and said, "You had way more trees than you needed, so at least someone who works for you likes Christmas. Anyway, Steve said the extra trees were stored in the hold."

"Movie!" Chris shouted and took a bite of his hot dog.

"Small bites, Chris, and chew it really well," Mia warned. Sam looked at the kid like he was a live bomb. He really did not need one of the boys choking on a hot dog.

Mia picked up a remote, and turned the wide screened TV on. She hit the right channel and played *Home Alone* for the boys who started laughing the minute they saw their favorite classic.

Then she got back to her subject as she tossed a few silk pillows to the boys so they could lay on them. "So anyway, Steve's bringing the tree and Devon, the Assistant Cruise Director, said he'd find the decorations that were set aside in case they were needed and I thought we could have a decorating party with the boys."

"I'm *good* at decorating," Charlie told him. "Can we get snow from the snow room to put on it?"

"No," Sam said and ignored the kid's crestfallen expression. Looking at Mia, he said, "You got my employees in on this?"

"Yep, and they were really great. Everyone was so anxious to help out the boss's wife."

Yeah, he bet they were. "You set me up."

"I really did." Mia grinned, patted his arm, then leaned over to pick up a hot dog. Layering it with mustard, she added, "Now all you have to do is enjoy it."

Enjoy Christmas trees and decorations and kid movies and two kids laughing and talking at pitches only dogs should be able to hear? Yeah. He'd get right on that.

"I don't—"

"Like Christmas. I know. But it's just a tree, Sam." She pushed her hair back from her face and held her hot dog out to him. "Want a bite?"

He shook his head and she grinned at him. "So the question is, are you going to disappoint the boys— and me—or are you going to pretend to be a Christmas elf?"

"Our elf went swimming in the toilet today," Charlie said around a bite of hot dog. "Chris said Buddy wanted to swim so Chris put him in the toilet cuz it's like a little pool for elfs."

"Elves," Mia corrected.

"Mommy used her hair dryer on him, but he was still wet, so he's going to get a tan out in the sun tomorrow."

"A tan," Sam repeated.

Chris piped up and added, "Mommy says elfs can't swim good so I shouldn't put him in the pool again."

"Good plan," Sam said, then took a breath and blew it out.

Elves in toilets. Christmas trees. Hot dogs. He looked at Mia and he was lost. Her green eyes were sparkling with suppressed laughter. She was really enjoying all of this. The shouts, the kids kicking their heels against the chairs, the movie turned up to a deafening level and his consternation at what

had happened to his nice, orderly world and his se-
duction plans.

What the hell was a man supposed to do with a
woman like that?

A knock on the door sounded again before he
could figure it out, and both boys shouted "Christmas tree!"

Mia just looked at him. Waiting.

He could leave. Do some work. Make some calls.
But he wasn't going to. He may have blackmailed
Mia into moving in, but it seemed, she was getting
him to do things he wouldn't normally do, too. And,
he thought, they both knew it. Shaking his head,
Sam said, "I'll let them in. And I want mustard on
my hot dog."

Eight

Three hours later, the boys were exhausted, the Christmas tree was beautifully decorated from the middle down and the scent of hot dogs was clinging to the air.

Mia smiled to herself. The evening had gone better than she'd hoped. Even though he'd been coerced into taking part in their festivities, Sam had come around. He'd put the lights on the tree, watched the kids hanging ornaments as high as they could reach and joined them for some chocolate chip cookies during the *Rudolph the Red-Nosed Reindeer* movie.

But the best part, she told herself, was seeing little Chris climb up on the couch to cuddle with his uncle and Sam automatically wrapping his arm around the boy. He probably hadn't even noticed when it had happened, but she had and Mia was still smiling to herself over it.

When Maya and Joe showed up to collect their kids, Joe scooped Chris into his arms and Maya took Charlie's hand in hers. Looking around at the detritus left behind by her children in what was usually a tidy, elegant space, Maya grinned.

"Seems like everyone had a good time," she said, looking directly at Sam.

"It was fun," Mia told her and bent to kiss Charlie goodbye.

"Thanks for watching them," Joe said. "It was nice having dinner and only cutting up my own meat."

Sam laughed and Mia beamed at him. Really, he'd been great with the kids and her heart was feeling so full, she might burst. This was what she'd hoped for in her marriage. What she wanted most in her life. And this, she told herself had been what she and everyone else had worried about. Being around Sam, spending time with him, had her falling in love with him all over again.

Yes, he was a little stern and so dedicated to his business he barely noticed life around him most of the time. But oh my when she did have his attention, when he was relaxed, he made her feel so much. Made her think about possibilities.

Made her remember how much she loved him.

Her heart did a tumble and roll in her chest and

she knew she was in trouble. She was supposed to be here to get the man she loved to sign divorce papers when all she really wanted was for him to stop her. For him to say he didn't want to split up. That he loved her and wanted to be with her always.

That he wanted this life they could have together. *And what were the chances of that happening?*

Slim, she told herself firmly. So what she had to do, was remember *why* she'd wanted the divorce. It hadn't been because she didn't love him. But because she was tired of being married all alone.

Maya's expression was wary, as if she couldn't really believe that any of this was happening and Mia couldn't blame her twin. She'd hoped of course, that Sam would go along with her plan to watch the kids and have a Christmas evening, but a part of her had been sure he'd find a way to disappear. After all, when they were together, disappearing had been his superpower.

He'd surprised her tonight and clearly her sister was a little stunned, too.

"Thanks again," Maya said, holding onto her oldest son while cradling her baby bump with her free hand. "We're taking these two off to bathe and go to bed."

"Good idea," Sam said, tucking both hands into his pockets. "We've all got mustard, ketchup and mac and cheese on us."

Maya laughed and winked at her sister. "So, a typical dinner. Good to know."

Joe headed for the door and Maya was right be-hind him. But when she got to the door, she paused as Charlie broke free of her grip and ran to Sam to hug him around the legs.

"Thanks Uncle Sam. That was great!"

Clearly a bit embarrassed, Sam gave the boy an awkward pat and said, "You're welcome."

Charlie grinned up at him, then darted back to his mother. "Is Buddy the Elf dry yet, Mom?"

"Let's go check," she said and gave Sam a nod and a slow smile before they left.

Mia closed the door behind them and leaned against the heavy panel. Amazing how two little kids could completely exhaust you in a matter of hours. As much as she loved her nephews, she was grateful for the sudden silence that dropped on the suite. Looking at Sam, she asked, "Should we call the kitchen, have someone come and take away the trays?"

"What?" He shook his head, then reached up to push both hands tiredly through his hair. "No. Let's not. They can come for them tomorrow. I've had enough of people for tonight."

"Me too," she said and moved away from the door to walk to him. He had mustard on his shirt, dried ketchup on his chin and a stray macaroni noo-dle stuck to his collar. Smiling, she reached up and plucked it off, then showed it to him. "A different look from those tailored suits of yours. I like it."

"How the hell—"

"No one knows," she said. "Get too close to children and you'll come away covered with all kinds of interesting things."

"How do they have so much energy?"

"Another mystery." Mia moved into him, wrapping her arms around his waist, laying her head on his chest.

His arms came around her and he rested his chin on top of her head. "Did you enjoy all of that?"

She leaned back to look up at him. "I really did. How about you? Were you completely miserable the whole time?"

Sam frowned at her. "You know I wasn't."

"Yeah, I know. I just wanted to hear you admit it."

"Fine. Here it is then." Taking a breath, he looked into her eyes and said, "I admit it. It was fun. Watching the kids put the ornaments on the tree—" he glanced across the room to where the brightly lit, artificial tree almost seemed to be leaning to one side because the kids had clumped everything together. Looking back into her eyes, he continued. "Hot dogs for dinner. The mac and cheese was good..."

She held up the one dried-up noodle. "So I noticed."

Sam snorted. "I even liked that movie—*Home Alone*?"

Stunned, she asked, "You've never seen that before?"

"Why would I?" He shrugged. "I don't do Christmas, remember?"

"Sometimes you amaze me."

"Thanks." One corner of his mouth quirked up. "Anyway, it wasn't as terrible as I thought it would be."

"High praise indeed," she said, then went up on her bare toes to plant a quick kiss on his lips. "And now... I think I need a shower as badly as the boys need their baths."

"Right there with you."

"That's what I was hoping," she murmured, staring into his eyes.

"What?"

"I said," Mia trailed her fingers down his shirt-front. "I was hoping you'd be right there with me, in the shower—unless you're too wiped out."

Slowly, a wide grin curved his mouth. "Yeah, I think I'm getting my second wind."

"Good to know," she countered and headed for his bedroom and the massive adjoining bath. "We'll use your bathroom. I think we're going to need the space."

In minutes, they had stripped and were walking into the enormous, connected bathroom. The wall of glass lining one side allowed for a really astonishing view of the moonlight-kissed ocean and the cloud-tossed, starry sky above it.

The tiled floor was heated and felt delicious as she walked unerringly toward the impressive, if a little scary, shower. It was completely made of glass and cantilevered to jut out from the side of the ship, so that she could literally look down at the ocean below while she showered. Naturally, the glass was treated so that the view was definitely only one-way. No one could see in. No one would know anyone was in that shower.

She turned to face Sam as he approached and her stomach jittered with expectation. There were no nerves between them. Only exploration. Mutual desire. Need.

Sam joined her in the middle of the shower, and said aloud, "Shower on."

Instantly, water, heated to the perfect temperature, erupted from six different showerheads placed at all different angles and heights. Surprised, Mia laughed and swiped wet hair from her face. "A voice-activated shower?"

He grinned at her. "Hands-free, so I can keep busy in other ways."

There were two dispensers attached to one wall and Sam reached for one of them, squirting body wash into his palm. The hot water pummeled them both as he lathered the soap then ran his hands all over Mia's body.

Slick. Slick and strong, each stroke of his hands drove her along the path she was so ready for. She rubbed her own palms over her soapy breasts then transferred that soap to Sam's chest, and smiled to herself when he sucked in a breath. Mia instantly reached for the dispenser herself and when her hands were soapy, she did to him exactly what he was doing to her.

She defined every muscle, every line of his amazing body and felt her eager response to him climb. Her right hand curled around his hard length and began to slide rhythmically. She watched his eyes, heard his tightly controlled groan and smiled to herself again.

The hot water continued to cascade across their skin and as they moved together, bodies skimming against each other, the heat in the shower intensified.

Yet it wasn't enough.

Sam called out, "Shower off," and the spray of water instantly stopped.

He picked her up and Mia sighed into his neck before running her lips and tongue along his throat. Her heartbeat thundered and her blood was racing. Sam's long legs carried them into the bedroom quickly and when he laid her down on the mattress, she reached her arms up for him.

"Just a minute," he murmured and reached for the bedside drawer. He grabbed a condom and in a second or two had sheathed himself before coming back to her. "We forgot last time," he whispered, "no sense pushing our luck."

"Right." A small curl of disappointment unwound in the pit of her stomach, but when Sam took one of her nipples into his mouth, that feeling was pushed to the back of her mind.

He joined her on the big bed and knelt down before sitting back on his haunches. Mia looked up at him and smiled as he reached for her. Lifting her easily, he settled her on his lap and Mia braced herself on her knees. She ran her hands through his still wet, silky black hair and leaned in to kiss him long and hard, letting her own need guide her.

Why was it that she never seemed to get enough of him? She wanted to keep touching him, to hold him, to have his mouth on hers and his body locked deep within. And on that thought, she rose up on her knees and then slowly lowered herself onto his erection. Inch by tantalizing inch, Mia tortured them both by moving as slowly as she could.

Until finally, Sam muttered thickly, "Enough!" His hands at her hips, he pulled her down hard, pushing himself high inside her.

Mia groaned, let her head fall back and then deliberately swiveled her hips, creating a delicious friction that reverberated all through her. And when she lifted her head to meet his gaze again, she saw fire in Sam's eyes.

"You recovered from being tired really well."

"Just what I was thinking about you," he said and leaned close enough to taste the pulse point at her throat.

Mia shivered and moved on him again. He hissed in a breath and dug his fingers harder into her hips. Guiding her movements, he set the rhythm they danced to and she raced to keep up. Her arms around his neck, she locked her gaze with his and when the first ripples of completion gathered in her like a storm, she welcomed them.

"Let go, Mia," he crooned. "Just let go."

"No," she insisted, her voice broken, halting. "Together. This time we go together."

"Stubborn woman," he muttered and made a fast move, flipping her onto the bed and covering her body with his.

He lifted her legs and hooked them on his hips, then leaning over her, he drove into her heat with such a quickness Mia's breath was lost. Her head tipped back onto the mattress and she stared blindly at the ceiling as he rocked his hips against hers in a frantic rhythm.

Mia felt his body tighten, his muscles flex and she knew that he was as close to shattering as she was. She fixed her gaze on his again and he stared back, just as determinedly.

"Together," he whispered, through gritted teeth.

"Now," she countered. "Please, *now.*"

"Now," he agreed and stiffened against her as her body splintered around his. They clung to each other like survivors of a shipwreck and when the tremors finally stopped, they collapsed together to ride out the storm.

Sam threw one arm across his eyes and waited for his heart rate to slow down to less than a gallop. Every time with Mia was like the first time. Every time with her only fed his hunger for *more* with her.

He dropped his arm away and turned his head to look at her. The satisfied smile on her face made him smile in return, though she couldn't see him. The woman was a mystery to him in so many ways. Whenever he felt as though he had her completely figured out, she threw another curveball that knocked him off kilter.

Most women he'd known would use those moments after sex to ply him with questions, or prod him to make promises he wasn't interested in keeping. But not Mia. From the first time they'd been together, she'd simply enjoyed that afterglow and had accepted what they had for what it was.

He was the one who'd proposed, though he knew she wasn't expecting it. *He* was the one who had taken that step though he'd known it wouldn't work out in the end. And now, here she was, forgetting about how he'd blackmailed her to get her into his bed and instead, enjoying this time together for however long it lasted.

"You're staring," she murmured.

"Guess I am," Sam admitted and she finally turned her head to look at him. Her mouth curved and her eyes shone as her red hair spilled across the white pillowcase. His heart fisted as he watched her. "You're beautiful, Mia."

She blinked and he could see she was surprised at the comment. Had he not told her before? Had he kept that to himself even when she took his breath away? Was it so hard for him to give a compliment?

"Okay, now you're scowling. What's going on, Sam?"

"Good question." He wasn't sure and he didn't like the feeling at all. Indecision was a foreign concept to him. And it made him uncomfortable enough that he shifted the conversation to her rather than him. Staring into her eyes, he blurted out, "I'm curious. Why'd you want the divorce in the first place?"

"What?"

"You heard me." He went up on one elbow. "I didn't get it then—oh, I wasn't surprised by it, but I didn't understand your reasoning for it and I still don't. We almost never argued. The sex was great. So what was the problem?"

Shaking her head, she turned on her side and propped herself up. "Let me answer that with a question. Do you remember my grandparents' sixtieth anniversary party?"

Thinking about that, he had to frown. "No, I don't."

"Yeah, that's because you didn't go." She pushed her hair back from her face. "You promised me that you'd be there, but at the last minute, you 'had' to fly to Florida for a meeting with Michael."

Sam's frown deepened. He remembered that now. The truth was, even after they'd gotten married, he'd focused on the company because he'd known even then that the business was all he could really count on. His marriage would end, eventually. But Buchanan Cruises would be there forever—as long as he was a good custodian. "Sometimes business has to come first."

"Uh-huh," she said. "But the party's only one example of you disappearing without thinking about how it affected me." She shrugged, but Sam could see she wasn't taking this conversation as lightly as she was pretending to.

Then she was talking again. "You could have taken a later flight, but that didn't occur to you."

"Mia, I have a company to take care of."

"You had a marriage to take care of, too," she reminded him. "You were always so busy, Sam. If we had dinner plans, it was because you had decided that we could be together. When I decided I wanted to buy myself a car—suddenly one was in the driveway."

He remembered that. Sam had bought her a fire-engine red SUV because it was the safest car on the market. "That was a good car."

"It was the car *you* thought I should have. Even though you knew that I'd already decided to get myself a VW."

"The SUV was safer."

"And not what I wanted," she countered, shaking her head. "You never listened. You simply pushed your way down my throat, expecting me to roll along."

Sam decided he really didn't care for this conversation.

"My fault too," she added quickly, "because I *did*

roll along. For a while. But being in love with you didn't mean I stopped having a mind of my own. Honestly, I think the real problem was that you never learned to bend. To give a little. Basically, Sam, I got tired of being all alone in our marriage. It's hard to be the one always giving and getting nothing in return."

He could see that and he didn't like having to admit that she was right.

"And I wanted kids, Sam," she said softly, her gaze locked on his. "I wanted a family with you— and you didn't."

It wasn't so much what she said as her expression when she said it. Sam could see the shadows of old pain in her eyes and knew that it hadn't been any easier for her to say all of this than it had been for him to hear it. He wanted to defend himself, damn it. He wanted to say that he'd known that he would be a lousy husband. That marriage to him was a losing bet right from the start. But that he'd married her anyway because he'd loved her.

He didn't say any of it though, because it felt to Sam as if he were trying to make excuses and he didn't do that. Ever. He took responsibility for his actions. Which was why he'd agreed to the divorce when she'd first broached the subject.

He'd failed. Not something he did often. Not something he really ever admitted to. Not something he was proud of. But his mistake—his duty to fix it.

"I'm not saying any of this to make you feel bad,

Sam," she said and reached out to lay her hand on his forearm.

He felt that soft, warm touch right down to his bones.

"I accepted that our marriage was over months ago and started making plans for my future." She smiled. "I'm not broken anymore."

Broken.

He hated the sound of that. She was so strong, so confident, he'd never even considered that he might have the power to break Mia Harper. Knowing he had was like a knife to the heart.

The darkness of the bedroom was only relieved by the moonlight beyond the glass wall. And in that pale wash of light, her eyes were shadowed and almost impossible to read. Maybe, he told himself, that was a good thing.

When they returned to Long Beach, he'd be signing those papers, as promised. The two of them would no longer be linked, in any way. She had plans, as she'd said many times, for her future, plans that didn't include *him.*

Suddenly, he wanted to know what they were.

"You keep talking about your plans," he said, initiating an abrupt change of subject. "What are they?"

"Why do you want to know?" she asked, honestly curious.

"So, when I *do* take an interest and ask a question, you're not happy?"

"Fair point," she said and he saw the quick flash

of a smile. "Okay. If you really want to know. I need you to sign those divorce papers soon because I have an appointment to keep on January twenty-fifth."

Now he was more curious than ever. "What kind of appointment?"

"At a sperm bank. I'm going to be a mother just as soon as I can arrange it."

Whatever he'd been expecting, that wasn't it. He was stunned. Okay, yes, he knew she wanted kids, but to do it on her own? Be impregnated by a stranger?

"Why?" he asked and sat up, drawing up one knee and resting his forearm on it. "Why would you do that?"

"Why wouldn't I?" she countered and sat up to face him. Both of them naked and not caring, they glared at each other for a long minute before Mia started talking again. "I wanted kids with you, but you shot that down."

All right, there was still some guilt left there. He lifted one hand and nodded. "I know. I should have told you where I stood before we married. It's not that I don't like kids. Your sister's boys are great. It's just that I'd be no better at being a father than I was at being a husband."

"That's crazy. You were great with the kids tonight."

"For three hours," he pointed out. "They weren't my kids."

"No, they weren't," she said. "And as much as I

love them, they're not mine, either. And I want my own children, Sam. Why should I wait to try to find someone else to love?"

He didn't like the sound of that, either. "What's the big rush?"

"I'm thirty years old and I don't want to wait until I'm forty to get started. That's okay for some women, but not for me." Shaking her head, she lifted her chin, took a deep breath and said, "That's why I'm taking my future into my own hands."

"To get pregnant by a nameless guy who left a sample in a cup." He couldn't believe this. "Doing this alone, Mia? Not exactly easy."

"Nothing worthwhile is easy," she said and shrugged. "And I won't be completely alone. I'll have my family. They're all behind me on this."

He knew she was right there. The Harper family would circle the wagons to protect and help one of their own and just briefly, he wondered what that must feel like. To be able to count on people.

"Yeah. You said *children*. You're going to do this more than once?"

"Hopefully. I've always wanted three kids."

Stunned, he asked, "Have you always wanted to do it alone?"

"Of course not. I wanted to do it with my husband."

He gritted his teeth to keep from saying the wrong thing.

"But the fact that I am alone isn't going to stop me."

His brain was buzzing with too many thoughts at once. He didn't even know what to say to all of this. Imagining Mia pregnant with another man's child hit him hard, leaving behind an ache in his heart and a knot in his gut. But surely insemination was easier to consider than picturing Mia naked in some other man's bed.

He shouldn't care, either way. He knew that. They weren't a couple anymore and really—they never had been. They were married, but they weren't a unit. They lived together but led separate lives. So why the hell was this bugging him so much?

Sam climbed off the bed and stalked across the room to the balcony doors. Tossing them open, he let the cold wind rush into the room. Instantly, Mia yelped and he glanced over his shoulder to see her grab the quilt off the bed and wrap it around her. She clutched it to her chest as she walked toward him. The wind lifted her hair and drifted her scent to him and that did nothing to ease his mind.

"Why is this bothering you so much?"

He pushed one hand through his hair, then scrubbed that hand across his face. "I don't know."

"Geez. Good answer."

"What do you want from me, Mia?"

"Just what I've always wanted from you, Sam. Honesty."

"You want honest? Okay, how's this?" This idea had just occurred to him a moment ago and now he found himself blurting it out.

"When we had sex the night of the storm, we didn't use a condom. Were you hoping you'd get pregnant then?" He kept his gaze fixed on hers and waited for the answer.

"Of course not." Her eyes went wide and in the moonlight, the insult stamped on her features was easy to read. "I wasn't thinking about protection any more than you were."

She had him there. That first night with her after months apart, a condom was the last thing on his mind. He'd been desperate to have her and he hadn't been capable of rational thought at all.

Still... "Okay, I grant you that. But you wouldn't have minded if you did get pregnant."

"You say that like it's some great shock to you. I've already taken steps to start my own family and that's why you signing those papers is so important. I don't want any custody questions later. But if I had gotten pregnant that night—no. I wouldn't have minded. Why would I mind getting pregnant by my *husband*?"

"And yet you keep saying we're not married."

"Oh for heaven's sake, Sam. I want kids. You know that. If I got pregnant the other night, of course I wouldn't care. But I also wouldn't have expected anything from *you*."

"Meaning..."

"Meaning," she said, "I would sign whatever you wanted, releasing you from child support or any other connection to my baby."

Hearing that he'd have been tossed aside once his usefulness was done wasn't easy to hear. "Just like that."

"You don't want children," she said. "I do."

He wouldn't be used. He wouldn't be discarded. He would, though, let her know where he stood on this.

Sam tipped her chin up with his fingertips. When her gaze locked with his, he said, "If you are pregnant because of that night…you might find that I'm not so easy to dismiss."

Nine

"Tell me something, Sam," Mia said, ignoring that last statement as she stared up into his eyes. "Why don't you want children? Why do you hate Christmas? You never would tell me before, but tell me now."

"Why would I do that?"

"Consider it part of our bargain," she said. "Once this ship docks we'll never see each other again. Don't you think I'm owed an explanation finally?"

"Maybe." He stared out at the darkness and she studied the tightness in his jaw as she waited. Finally, after what seemed forever, he started talking, his voice low and dark.

"Christmas doesn't mean anything to me because

it never did," he muttered thickly. "Decorations...
just empty gestures. Like putting a mask over the
ordinary to pretend it's special even though it's not."

"I don't understand," Mia said softly, though her
heart was already breaking a little.

He glanced at her. "My father was busy with his
wives, then his girlfriends." He snorted as if choking out a laugh at his own pitiful memories. "There
was no Christmas at my house. No Santa. For sure,
no elves. The housekeeper put up a tree and some
garland and crap, but it was still an empty house."

It was so hard for Mia to hear this. To imagine
the boy he'd once been, alone and forgotten, watching the world celebrate without him.

"It sounds like the housekeeper tried," she offered,
though she knew it was a lame attempt.

"Maybe," he said with a shrug. "But all it accomplished was defining the emptiness." He turned
to look at her and her breath caught at the glint of
old pain in his eyes. "Garlands and trees and all the
other holiday crap doesn't mean anything to me because it was never special. Never a true celebration,
so I don't have them. But not having decorations up,
only reminds me of their lack. So yeah, no winning
at Christmas time for me."

"It doesn't have to be that way." Mia reached for
him, but let her hand fall without touching him. "We
could have made new memories together, Sam."

"Empty is all I know," he muttered and looked
back out at the ocean. Moonlight peeked out from be-

hind the clouds and painted the foam on the waves a pale silver. "And trust me. You don't want a man who was raised by my father, being a parent to your kids."

"You're wrong. About all of it, Sam."

He didn't look at her and maybe that was best for both of them. At the moment, her heart ached for him but she was sure he wouldn't appreciate any semblance of pity or sorrow. And at the same time she wanted to shriek because he'd given up on them because of things that had happened to him before they'd ever known each other.

"I'm sorry Sam," she said.

"Don't want your sympathy."

"That's too bad." Mia reached up and touched his cheek gently. "Because I do feel sorry for that little boy. But now, I'm furious with the grown man."

"What? Why?"

"Because you let that lonely child decide your whole life. You wrapped yourself in the past so tightly that you can't even see a future, let alone build one."

Shaking her head, Mia said, "You should have trusted me, Sam. Together we might have found a way."

"This is crazy, Mia."

The following day, Mia's mind was still whirling with everything she and Sam had talked about the night before. And dealing with the family at the moment was dancing on her last nerve.

"No, it's not," she argued, meeting her twin's worried gaze. "And it's really not worth an *intervention*." She glanced from her mother to her father to Maya, then sat back and folded her arms over her chest.

Mia loved her family, but sometimes they didn't make it easy. Maya had invited her to come over for coffee and doughnuts—something everyone knew Mia wouldn't refuse. But when she walked into the suite, Maya and her parents were at the table, Joe had taken the kids to the snow room and Merry was on the computer via FaceTime.

They all had something to say about her relationship with Sam. But gathering everyone together to form a united wall was a little much, even for them. And all because she'd moved into Sam's suite.

"Don't think of it like that, honey," her mother said and reached over to pat her hand.

"That's exactly what it is, Mom." Mia looked at her father. In a houseful of women, Henry Harper had always been the voice of reason. "Dad, you can't really be okay with this."

He glanced at his wife, then said, "I don't want to see you get hurt again, Mia. But it's your life and you should run it your way. Your mother and sisters just want to talk to you. They're worried, is all."

"I'm not." Merry's voice came from the laptop open on the table.

Mia looked at her. "Thank you for your sanity."

"You're not helping, Merry," Maya said, then

looked at her twin. "She's in love. Again. And not thinking about what that means."

Mia glanced at her twin. "I'm not an idiot, Maya. I love him, but I'm not expecting anything from him anymore." Especially after last night.

Once Sam had told her his secrets, he'd kept his distance from her—just like old times. The walls were down and now he was more defensive than ever.

"That's where you're making your mistake," Merry said and everyone looked at the computer screen.

"What do you mean?"

Sighing a little, Merry said, "Honey, you love Sam. But instead of fighting for what you wanted, you walked away."

"Um, he's the one who walked away, Mer."

"No, honey. You're the one who asked for the divorce. He just agreed."

Huh. That was true.

She hadn't considered it like that before, but Merry was right.

"If you want Sam, tell him," Merry said.

"And have him say no thanks? Yeah, that doesn't really sound like a good time."

"Mia, you don't know that's what he'll say unless you try it. If you love him, say so. See what happens. If he's not interested, you'll be no worse off than you are right now."

Maybe she had a point, but it was a step that Mia hadn't considered taking. Being Sam's lover again was supposed to be a short-time thing. She'd gone into it knowing that no matter how good it was, there wouldn't be a future for them. But what if there could be?

Maya leaned in closer to the screen. "What kind of feminist are you anyway?"

"Oh, stop it," Merry said, waving that off. "This is love, Maya, and all bets are off."

"Really? Why would you want a man who didn't want *you*?"

Merry laughed. "Since you guys called home to tell me that Sam and Mia are shacking up—I think we can reasonably assume that he *does* want her."

Maya grimaced, but said, "Okay, fine. But I don't trust him."

"Not up to you."

"It's not up to either of you," their mother said and caught everyone's attention.

Emma smiled at her husband then looked from one to the other of her daughters. "Your father made me see that as much as I want to protect Mia from being hurt again, it's not my decision to make. And it's not yours, either, girls. This is all up to Mia." She looked at her. "You know your own mind, Mia. You'll do what's best for you. And *we*," she glanced at everyone else in turn, "will support you no matter what you decide."

Quite a concession from her mother, Mia thought, then wished she actually knew what to do. That got Merry speaking again.

"Sweetie, stop thinking so hard and start feeling. Yes, you were unhappy in your marriage and I'm sorry about that. But maybe now, you're ready to fight for what you want."

"Why should I have to fight?" Mia asked. "He either loves me or he doesn't."

Her mother spoke up then. "Honey, sooner or later, you realize that everything worth having is worth fighting for."

Mia grabbed a doughnut, took a bite and only half listened as her family continued to argue and talk about her life, without *her*.

It didn't matter though, because her older sister's words were echoing inside her mind. Mia hadn't really fought for her marriage. Stood up for herself. Demanded that he pay attention. She'd simply given up on ever reaching Sam and had asked for a divorce. Sam hadn't fought either, but now, she knew enough about how he was raised to know that he wasn't used to being loved. And maybe she'd done exactly what he'd been expecting her to do all along.

Well, that was irritating. There was just nothing worse than being predictable.

"We're docking in Hawaii today, Merry," their mother said. "So we'll have a few days here and then fly home."

The trip was moving on. Soon her parents would be gone and not long after that, the ship would be back in Long Beach and this whole interlude would be over.

Mia could either go back to her life not knowing what might have happened if she'd only spoken up. Or, she could take a chance, tell Sam she loved him and maybe get everything she ever wanted.

When his cell phone rang, Sam looked at the screen, rolled his eyes and answered. "Michael. Everything all right?"

"That's what I was calling to ask you," his brother said. "How're things going with Mia?"

There was a loaded question, he thought. Sam had been up and out of the suite before Mia woke up because last night's conversation was still running through his mind and he wasn't in the mood to continue it.

His sleep had been haunted with the kind of images that would probably keep him from sleeping for the rest of his life. Mia. Pregnant with a baby that wasn't his. Raising kids on her own—unless of course, she married some other guy and then she'd be having *his* babies and Sam would go on as he had been.

Alone. Wasn't that better, though, he asked himself. He'd already proven that he couldn't be the kind of husband Mia wanted and deserved.

"That doesn't sound good," Michael said and snapped his brother's attention back to the conversation.

"Let it go, Michael."

"Damn it, Sam," the other man said, clearly exasperated. "This was the perfect opportunity for you to get past what our dear father did to your brain and have a real life."

Sam scowled at the phone. What he did not need was a pitying lecture from his younger brother. "I have a life, thanks. And it runs just the way I want it to."

"Alone. Forever."

"I'm only alone when I want to be," Sam argued.

"Great," Michael said. "So you're going to be a man just like our father. A long string of temporary women coming and going out of your life and not one of them meaning a damn."

He didn't like the sound of it, but the truth was, that was what he'd been raised to be.

"Is there a reason you called besides a chance to hammer at me?" Sam demanded.

"Yeah. I wanted to let you know the new Clipper ship is taking shape. They've got most of it built out and it looks like they'll beat their own deadline."

"Finally," Sam muttered. "Good news."

"Even better news? They're thinking she'll be ready to take her first passengers in another six months."

"Good timing. Ready for the summer sailing crowd."

"That's what I thought. If this one works as well as we think it will, we should put the next Clipper ship on the routes leaving Long Beach."

"I think so too. Lots of people would want to take that kind of ship to Hawaii or Panama…"

"And since we agree on that, I'm going to push my luck," Michael said. "Don't blow this second shot with Mia, Sam. You don't want to be Dad, the sequel."

When his brother hung up, Sam stared out at the sea and told himself that his brother just didn't get it. But as he stood there at the bow of the ship, watching the waves slash at the boat, an idea began to form in his mind.

It was a damn good idea, too. He hoped to hell it would work out better this time—and he thought that maybe it could.

All he had to do was convince Mia.

Once they were in port and docked in Honolulu, the passengers fled the luxurious ship to explore the island. Mia's family was no exception. She watched her sister's family, along with their parents, take off for a day on land. She hadn't gone with them, because she needed to see Sam. To decide if she should try Merry's advice or not.

The notion of risking her heart again wasn't easy. Living through losing Sam once had nearly killed her. If she allowed herself to hope and lost again… the pain would be so much worse.

Still, it wasn't in Mia's nature to give up, so it had cost her to admit that her marriage was not what she had hoped it would be. But she'd finally come to terms with it and now, she was supposed to take a chance again? She didn't know if she was willing to or not.

"You look deep in thought."

That voice reverberated throughout her body. Mia's heartbeat jumped as she slowly turned around to look at Sam. Surprising to see him in khakis, a dark green, short-sleeved shirt and casual brown shoes. She was so accustomed to seeing him in a suit, she hardly knew what to make of casual Sam.

"No business meetings today?"

"No," he said and moved to stand beside her at the railing. In port, they could watch surfers and day sailors on their little skiffs with jewel-toned sails. The view, complete with huge white clouds and a heartbreakingly blue sky, was like a living painting.

"Where's the family?" he asked, and glanced around, as if expecting Maya to come growling around a corner.

Mia laughed a little. "They all went ashore. Mom and Dad for shopping, Maya, Joe and the kids to hit the beach."

"But you didn't go with them." His gaze was fixed on hers now and Mia thought that his eyes were an even nicer view than the one she had just admired.

"No, I wanted to stay here. Maybe…" she paused. "Talk to you again."

Nodding, he leaned his forearms on the railing and glanced at her. "Don't you think we said enough last night?"

"I don't know," she admitted. And that was part of the problem. Last night, he'd let down some of the walls surrounding him and maybe she was hoping he'd open up some more. Really let her in. If he didn't, would she push? Sex with Sam was wonderful, but it didn't clear up the situation either, it only confused things further.

"Well." He straightened up and laid both hands on her shoulders.

Heat swept through her and Mia felt powerless against it.

"Why don't we go ashore, too?" Sam asked. "Do the tourist thing. We can talk while we go."

Like they had before on the cruise when they'd met.

"That sounds good," she said.

"Great." He smiled at her and took her hand. "Let's go."

Sam took her to every spot they'd visited the year before. From the beaches on the north shore to the shops and restaurants in the city. In the rental car, they were out for hours, and it seemed that once away from the ship, the tension between them slipped away. They laughed and talked as they had when first getting to know each other and when they stopped for lunch Mia smiled at him and said, "Thanks for this."

"You're welcome. But it was for me, too," Sam

admitted. "Seeing you again made me remember a lot of things I forced myself to forget."

She picked up her iced tea and took a sip. "That's the difference between us. I didn't want to forget."

"Didn't say I wanted to," Sam countered. "I said I forced myself to."

"Why?"

He laughed at that. "Seriously. Why? Because we weren't together anymore, Mia. Remembering was pointless. Painful."

"Was it?" she asked. "Painful, I mean."

He gritted his teeth and chose his words carefully. "Did you really believe that breaking up meant nothing to me?"

"It didn't seem to bother you," she said quietly, so that others in the tiny restaurant wouldn't overhear.

The restaurant was very small and obviously designed to attract tourists as there were grass skirts tacked to the walls and tiki torches along the patio outside. But the servers were friendly, the views were beautiful and the food smelled delicious.

"What would have been the point of indulging pain? It was over," he said, remembering the look on her face when she'd asked him for a divorce. He'd taken the hit because he'd been prepared for it from the moment they'd taken their vows. Sam was expecting the marriage to end, so pain wasn't unexpected.

"If you're so okay with this, why didn't you just sign those divorce papers the first day I gave them to you?"

Yeah, he didn't have a ready answer for that question. He wasn't even sure *he* knew the reason he'd delayed. A little self-torture?

"Never mind," she said, waving one hand in the air as if to erase her question. "Let's just have lunch and enjoy the rest of the day."

A tiny smile tugged at one corner of his mouth. "You mean, we should enjoy 'the now'?"

Her gaze snapped up to his and she grinned briefly. "Okay, yes. Let's enjoy the now."

"Welcome to my world," he said and lifted his glass of beer in a toast.

She did the same. Then there was silence for a couple of long seconds while Sam watched her, indulging himself by looking into her green eyes and admiring the fall of that red hair. Finally, he heard himself say, "Come to dinner with me tonight."

She blinked at him and he could see the surprise in her eyes. "Dinner?"

He shrugged, to downplay what he was feeling. "Why not keep enjoying the now?"

Mia looked at him for what seemed forever and he knew she was trying to figure out what he was thinking. He wished her luck with that, because even he couldn't make sense of his jumbled thoughts at the moment. But finally, she nodded.

"Okay. Dinner."

And after that, he promised himself, they'd celebrate by doing what they did best.

* * *

"Have I told you yet, that you look beautiful?"

Mia smiled at Sam. "You mentioned it, but thank you. It's nice to hear."

She was wearing a sleeveless, sunshine-yellow dress with a short, full skirt and a pair of taupe, three-inch heels. She'd left her hair down and the humidity had zapped some dormant curls into life.

Sam of course, looked gorgeous in a black suit with a white dress shirt and a deep, magenta tie.

And the setting was both lovely and curious. The Sunset Cliffs restaurant was just what the name implied. It sat high on a cliff side with a breathtaking view of the ocean and the beach far below them. The stone patio was dotted with a dozen cloth-covered tables—empty now—that each boasted a hurricane lamp where candle flames danced in a soft, warm breeze.

And at sunset, she remembered, the view was staggering as the sun turned the ocean orange and gold, scarlet and purple. She remembered everything about the night she was last here, a year ago when Sam had brought her here to propose.

She could see it all in her memory as clearly as if it had happened the night before. But she didn't look at it. Instead, she watched Sam and wondered why he'd brought her to this particular restaurant. She wouldn't have called him a sentimental man, so why?

Sipping at her glass of crisp, white wine, Mia

tilted her head to one side and studied him until he shifted under that steady stare.

"What?"

She shook her head. "It's just—I'm glad you brought me here for dinner."

"Best restaurant on the island."

"And is that why we're here?"

"No," he admitted, then shifted to look out at the horizon where the sun was beginning to dazzle. "We took that trip down memory lane today, I thought we should finish it up right."

That made her sad and happy, which was just ridiculous and a total sign of how messed up she was over this situation. Was the restaurant just a memory to him?

Or was it that he wanted to experience that night all over again? Was there more to his motivation in bringing her here than he was admitting? She'd like to think so, but how could she be sure?

"Well, if you wanted to really relive that night we were here," she said, with a knowing smile, "there should be other diners at the tables."

He glanced around, then looked back at her and shrugged. "Buying out the patio just for the two of us seemed like a good idea. This way we can talk and not have people listening in."

Huh. What was it he wanted to talk about? Was he going to suggest they stay together and have those babies she wanted so badly? Had he realized that life without her wasn't nearly as good as life *with* her?

Oh, Mia really wanted to think so. And in spite of her efforts to keep it in check, her heartbeat sped up, racing with possibilities.

Maybe Merry was right. Maybe this was the time to tell him that she loved him. That she didn't really want the divorce. She wanted him. And a family.

"What did you want to talk about?" she asked instead.

He reached across the table for her hand and folded it into his. "I wanted to tell you that these last few days with you have been…"

"… I think so, too."

"Good," he said, nodding, keeping his gaze fixed on hers. "Because since last night, when we talked, I've been thinking about a lot of things."

"Okay…" There went her heartbeat again as hope rose within in spite of everything.

The waiter brought their meals and Sam released her hand and waited until the man had left again before he started speaking. "When you said you were going to a sperm bank," he admitted, "I didn't like it."

She hadn't expected *that*, so she said, "I'm sorry, but that's my choice."

"I understand that." Sam lifted one hand for peace. "I do. And I get why you've decided to do it. But hearing your plan started me thinking and kept me up most of the night. Today, something occurred to me and that's been racing through my brain until I can't think of anything else."

"What are you talking about, Sam?" She held her breath because hope was a dangerous thing. Not enough hope and life wasn't worth living. Too much and you were setting yourself up for constant disappointment.

Their dinners were ignored as they stared at each other, while the sky went lavender and the dancing candle flame reflected in their eyes.

"I'm talking about what happened the night of the storm."

Confused, she asked, "You mean when we had sex?"

"Unprotected sex," he corrected.

Now her stomach jittered in time with her galloping heartbeat. She didn't know where he was going with this, but she really hoped she would like where they ended up.

"You could be pregnant right now," he said tightly.

She hadn't allowed herself to think about the chances of that happening. Because the truth was, she would love being pregnant with Sam's baby. True that hadn't been the plan. But if she were pregnant with Sam's child, she wouldn't be disappointed. Even if it meant she still wouldn't have Sam.

"I suppose so." Instinctively, Mia's right hand dropped to her belly as if to protect the child that might be there.

"When I realized that, I decided something else." He paused, reached for her hand again and held on. "You want kids," he said. "Have mine."

She gasped. Had she heard him right? Of course she had. She wasn't deaf. She was just…stunned. Had he brought her back to this special place to propose again? To renew what they'd promised each other a year ago?

"Are you serious?"

"Why not?" He held her hand tighter, as if half-afraid she'd pull away before he was finished. He didn't have to worry, Mia thought. Now that he'd started, she had to hear the rest of his plan.

"We're still married, Mia."

"Yes, but—"

"We're good together."

"Okay…" Still confused, still hopeful, Mia told herself to wait. To keep hoping.

"So have my children," Sam said. "Stay married to me."

"You want us to be together again? To have a family?"

"That's what I'm saying."

"And how will it be different this time?" she asked.

"You'll have the kids you want."

Slowly, the air in her balloon of hope began leaking out.

"I will," she mused. "Not *we*."

"Mia, I've told you already," he explained. "I don't know how to be a father. All I do know, I learned from watching my father and believe me, that's not a role model you want to emulate.

"I told you some of it last night. Understand that my father was a bastard and his kind of parenting is all I know."

"You're not him, Sam."

"That's the thing," he admitted. "I don't know if I am or not and it doesn't seem fair to some innocent kid to take the chance. I'm just not good with kids."

She hated hearing him say that because it wasn't true. Mia had seen him with Maya's children. And the boys loved him. Kids were always good judges of people. If they loved Sam, then he was better with kids than he believed he was.

"Yes you are. Charlie and Chris love you. So do Merry's kids."

Sam released her hand and sat back. His gaze stayed on hers. "That's different. Being an uncle doesn't require the same amount of patience and— never mind, I'm not going to get into this again."

"Afraid I might convince you?"

He shook his head. "Don't make what I'm offering something it's not."

"Then what is it, Sam? Be specific."

"It's simple. We stay married. You get the kids you want. And we go on as we were before."

And with that, she thought, the balloon was flat and dead.

"No, Sam," she said and felt him loosen his grip on her hand. "I can't do that. What we had was an empty marriage and it almost cut my heart out."

Frowning, he argued, "Come on Mia, it wasn't that bad. We got along great. We had a good time."

"When you were there," she said softly. "But you stayed away as much as you could. Now you want to go back to the same thing that hurt me so badly? And worse yet, you want to add children into the mix— kids who would have their hearts damaged because their father wasn't fully there for them."

A chill dropped across the surface of his eyes. "I would make sure they had everything they needed."

"Except love." Mia sighed and looked out at the sunset, sorry to see the glorious colors had already faded and the ocean was going dark. "We missed it."

"What? Missed what?"

"The sunset," she said, though her heart was breaking. "We were arguing and we missed the beautiful show."

"It was a sunset," he said. "There's another one tomorrow."

She looked at him and really hoped she didn't start crying. She did not want to do that until she was alone and could really give in to it.

"Don't you see, Sam? Missing that sunset is a metaphor for what our lives would be like if I agreed to your plan."

"What the hell are you talking about?"

"If we got back together, doing the same thing that didn't work before, we'd miss the beauty."

"What beauty?"

"Of family," she said. "Of love. Of really being together."

"Mia…"

"No, Sam, let me finish." She looked at him, staring into those blue eyes of his until she felt steady enough to say, "I love you, Sam. I always have. Probably always will."

"That's a good thing, Mia."

"It should be," she agreed. "But I can't set myself up for more pain when I know that nothing has changed. You still believe that marriage is a nightmare and I still want a family."

He leaned in toward her. "I can give you that family, Mia."

Yes, he could, but he didn't see the whole picture. He would hold himself back from her, and from any kids they had. And that sounded like an empty life.

"It's tempting, Sam. So very tempting because I love you so much. But I can't do it. I deserve more," she said softly. "*We* deserve more. Don't you see, Sam? If you had children and never shared yourself with them, then you would be doing exactly what your dad did to you. You say you don't want to risk being him, but this …offer, is exactly that."

He stiffened and she knew she'd struck a chord. "You don't want that, do you Sam?"

"Of course not."

"I'm sorry. But I can't go back to having to fight for any scrap of attention from you. And I will not put my children through that."

"And that's it." It wasn't a question.

"That's it," she said sadly, then she picked up her purse. "If you don't mind, I'm not really hungry anymore. You stay. I'll take a cab back to the ship."

"Don't be ridiculous." He stood up, called the waiter over, handed the man a couple hundred dollars and told him to keep the change.

They walked out together—but separate—and Mia knew that's how they would always be.

It broke her heart all over again.

Ten

Sam drove in silence. What the hell could he say? He slanted a sideways glance at Mia and told himself that he'd tried. He'd offered her a life, the children she wanted, but it hadn't been enough.

The silence stretched on until it became a huge presence. A third passenger in the car, impossible to ignore and just as impossible to address.

From the corner of his eye, he saw Mia clutching her brown leather purse on her lap as if it were a lifeline. She sat poker straight and kept her gaze fixed on the road in front of them.

Man, this day had gone to hell fast.

At a stop light, his fingers drummed on the steering wheel, but he stopped when she said, "I'll move back to Maya's suite tonight."

He cursed under his breath and wished—hell, he didn't even know what he wished anymore. All he did know was that he wasn't going to send her back to sleeping on Maya's couch. They might not share a bed anymore, but there were two bedrooms in his suite. No matter how hard it would be, being around her and not touching her, damned if she would move out.

"No you won't." He turned to look at her and found her gaze locked on him.

"Sam—"

"Let me finish." The light changed and he stepped on the gas. Steering through the traffic, headed for the port, he said, "You can stay in the second bedroom. There's no reason for you to go back to Maya's couch."

"I'll be fine," she said, her voice determined.

"Yeah, but why should you have to just be fine?" He shook his head, but kept watching the road. "You can even lock the bedroom door if you feel like you need to."

"That's not it," she argued and he believed her. "I just don't want to make this harder on either of us than it has to be."

"Right. But do you really want to talk to Maya about why you're moving back?"

"No," she admitted and her body slumped, her

head dropping to the head rest. "I really don't. Not tonight."

"So stay." He felt her gaze on him and sighed. "Damn it, Mia, we're adults. I can be in the same room with you without making a move. And I think you're capable of saying no, even if I did."

"I know that. I told you, it's not about that. It's just—" She shifted in her seat so she was facing him. "I don't want it to be awkward between us now, Sam. And staying in your suite, seeing each other all the time, but not being together anymore—not even temporarily—will just make things that much harder to deal with."

"Relax, Mia. If you can handle it, so can I." He scowled at the thought, but said, "We go back to being what we were to each other when the cruise started. And when we get to the ship, I'll sign the damn papers for you. Sharing a suite doesn't have to be intimate. We'll avoid each other when we can and that should be good enough."

Though he was sure as hell going to miss being with her. Having the right to touch her. To hold her.

He already felt the loss of her as he would a limb and the real torture hadn't even begun yet.

"You'll sign the papers before we get back to Long Beach?"

He threw a quick glance at her. "Is there any point in waiting?"

"No," she said softly, "I suppose not."

"Okay then. This isn't anything new to us, Mia."

Though it was. Because he had offered her family. Kids. Everything he'd thought—hoped—she'd wanted. And she'd turned him down. That truth sank like a stone in the pit of his stomach. "We'll get through it."

And the silence crept back, settling down between them and this time, each of them hid behind the silence and were grateful for it.

For two days, Sam was like a ghost, slipping in and out of the suite at all hours and somehow managing to avoid seeing Mia completely. Clearly, he was doing everything he could to make it easier on both of them.

She didn't know whether to be angry about that or to leave him a thank-you note.

It was hard not seeing him, but it would have been so much harder to spend time with him and know that now, it was truly over. But God, she missed him so much.

"He asked you to stay married."

She looked at Maya. "Yes."

"And have kids."

"Yes."

"And you said no."

Mia took a deep breath, turned her head on the poolside chaise and said, "Yes. We've been over this a dozen times in the last two days already. For God's sake, Maya, why can't you let this go? Can't you see I really don't want to talk about it anymore?"

"Well, I'm still stunned. He stepped up, Mia. He agreed to kids."

"Yes, but he didn't agree to being part of that family he offered to build with me." And that still stung.

Ever since Mia had told her family that it was really over between her and Sam, Maya had been doing interrogations that the CIA would have been proud of.

"But you're still staying in his suite."

Mia groaned dramatically. "Maya, I beg you…"

"With no fun stuff."

"None." Mia sighed. Her twin was not getting past this anytime soon. But then, neither was Mia. And oh, how she missed the fun stuff with Sam. Every time she took a shower now, she remembered being with him, his hands sliding over her skin, caressing her breasts until she was mindless with need.

But strangely, even more than the sex, she missed having coffee with him in the morning. Missed laughing with him. Missed curling up next to him on the bed—until he stretched out his arms and legs in his sleep and nearly pushed her off the mattress. She missed laying out on their private deck holding hands and watching the stars. Missed…oh hell.

She just missed *him*.

"Did you know he took the boys up to the bridge yesterday?" Maya smiled and shook her head as if she still couldn't believe it herself.

Mia was stunned. Sam had spent time with the boys without her nudging him? "He did?"

Maya nodded and added, "He even got the Captain to let them take turns steering the ship. I've got to say, I'm glad I didn't know that the boys were in charge, even if it was only for a minute or two."

Mia's heart squeezed. "He didn't tell me."

"Well," Maya pointed out, "you did say you two aren't even talking now."

"No, we're not. In fact, I've hardly seen him in two days."

"Well, the boys were so excited after all of that, he and Joe took them for ice cream."

"What?" Mia shook her head as if she hadn't heard her sister right. That was so unlike Sam, she didn't know what to make of it. And in the end, it only made her feel worse, knowing that he was so good with kids—seeing that he was good with them—and he didn't realize it.

"I know," Maya agreed. "Shock time. That's one of the reasons I keep asking you about what happened. I mean, this sounds like a man who loves you."

The surprises just kept coming. "I can't believe you're defending Sam."

"Yeah, it's stunning to me, too." Maya tugged her hat brim a little lower onto her forehead. "You know how furious I was when you guys broke up?"

"Yeah," Mia said wryly. "I remember the fury and some mention of putting a curse on him."

Maya ignored that. "What I didn't tell you was the reason I was so mad? I *liked* Sam. And when he hurt you, I was furious at myself because I hadn't seen it coming."

Mia smiled at her twin, reached out and grabbed her hand for a quick squeeze. As irritating as family could be, Mia couldn't imagine her life without a twin who was so fiercely defensive of her.

But Maya wasn't finished. "And then we come on this ship and I watch him watching you and I'm pretty sure he loves you and then it all blows up again and he still loves you. And he's good to my kids. So I'm furious all over again."

They had all been on a roller coaster for far too long. The adrenaline rushes alone were exhausting. And Mia had cried herself out so that she woke every morning feeling dehydrated.

"You really need to dial it down, Maya. I know you're upset and I love you for it, but that baby you're carrying needs peace and quiet."

"Then he's coming to the wrong house," Maya said with a half laugh.

They sat beneath a red-and-white striped umbrella and watched everyone in the pool from the safety of shade. The breeze was lovely and the cruise would be short as the ship made its way to Kauai for two days. For the first time since boarding the ship, Mia was wishing the cruise was over. But there was still a week to go before they were home again. Would she make it through another week in that suite with Sam?

Mia was thankful that their parents had flown home the night before, ready to get back to work at the bakery. At least, she only had Maya's sympathy and outrage to deal with.

"I know you don't want to move back to our suite," Maya was saying, "and I get it, since just sitting on that couch hurts my back. But if you really don't want to stay with Sam, maybe you could take over Mom and Dad's suite."

Mia shook her head. "No good. I already checked. The suite was booked a week ago. Someone taking the trip to L.A. and then back again on a different ship."

"Well then, maybe you should take that as a sign."

"A sign of what?"

Maya shrugged. "Maybe the universe *wants* you and Sam to work this out and that's why it's keeping you together."

"The universe can butt out. Besides, I'm sorry," Mia said, turning to face her twin. "Aren't you the one who was telling me to run fast, run far from Sam just a few days ago?"

"I was," Maya admitted with a gracious nod. "And I changed my mind."

"As historic as that is," Mia commented, "I don't think talking is going to change anything."

Maya sighed. "Fine. I'll stop now."

"Thank you."

"After I say—"

"Maya…"

"After I say that I'm on your side in this, Mia."

She sighed and smiled. No matter what, she could

count on her sister. Her whole family, for that matter. So she would keep doing her crying in private so she wouldn't worry them. And then on the twenty-fifth, Mia would begin her journey toward a family of her own and Sam would be only a memory.

A wonderful, haunting, memory.

"Mrs. Buchanan?"

She turned to face the waiter standing beside her chaise. "Yes?"

"Mr. Buchanan asked that this be delivered to you at noon." He held out an envelope and when Mia took it, he turned and went back to work.

"Wow," Maya said. "He *really* doesn't want to talk."

Mia ignored her, opened the envelope and pulled out the single sheet of paper. Sam's bold, handwriting sprawled across the page.

Mia—I took an early flight out this morning. I'm headed to Bermuda on business. The suite is yours, so enjoy it.

It was good to be with you again. However briefly.
Be happy.
Sam.

"He's gone," Mia whispered.

Maya snatched the paper from her suddenly nerveless fingers. "He left? Without a word?"

"He sent word, Maya. You're holding it."

"Yeah, but come *on*. He couldn't look you in the eye to tell you he's leaving?"

"It's over," Mia whispered, finally accepting that

Sam didn't want what she did. Sam didn't feel what she did.

"Well, look out," her sister grumbled. "I'm changing my mind about him again."

"Don't," Mia said, looking at her twin. "Just accept it for what it is. Sam and I just weren't meant to be, I guess."

And saying that out loud ripped at Mia's heart. She'd let herself hope and even though that particular balloon was now flat and empty, it was hard to let go of it completely. But then, she had years ahead of her to face the emptiness that was waiting for her.

So she'd build her own family, love her own children and dream about what might have been if Sam had only trusted himself as much as she'd trusted him.

Sam stayed in Bermuda for two weeks. He spent most of his time at the shipyard, consulting with the builders, going over every detail of the new build.

He buried himself in work so that he didn't have time to think about Mia and how silent his life felt without her in it.

He stood at the window of the house the Buchanans kept on the island. Sam's grandfather had built the house, saying that he spent so much time there with ship builders, he needed his own place rather than a hotel. And then Sam's father had used it—as a place to bring the long string of women he'd been involved with.

But for one week every year, Sam and Michael had been together at this house. Every summer, the boys had a week to explore, to play, to be the brothers their parents had kept them from being. So there were good memories here for Sam. And he tried to focus on them, to keep the thoughts of Mia at a distance.

It didn't really work.

He hadn't expected to miss her so much. But he did. Waking up next to her, talking over coffee, listening to her laugh. Hell, he even missed how she shoved him over in the middle of the night and fought him for blankets.

And he remembered that night with the boys, decorating a Christmas tree, and how Mia had shone brighter than the twinkling white lights. For the first time in his life, Christmas decorations had been... beautiful.

Though he kept her out of his mind during the day, at night in his sleep, she was there. Always. Her sighs. Her smiles. The way she touched him and the way she came apart when he touched her. He woke up every morning, dragging, his mind cloudy, his chest tight as if he'd been holding his breath all night. And maybe he had been.

All he knew for sure was that getting over Mia was going to take years.

"You look lost in thought."

Sam turned and saw his younger brother standing in the doorway. He'd never been so glad to see anyone.

"I am—or was. Now that you're here, maybe that'll stop."

Michael moved into the main room, walked to the wet bar on the far wall and grabbed two beers from the under-the-counter fridge. He carried one to Sam, then opened his own.

"So what thoughts are you trying to get rid of?" He looked at the ceiling, tipped his head and said, "Hmmm. Let's think. Could it be, Mia?"

"Knock it off," Sam said, opened his beer and took a sip. "Didn't I just say I was glad I could stop thinking?"

"Okay, I'll think for you," Michael said and dropped into a chair. "I think you miss Mia. I think you had a great time on the ship and I think you didn't want to leave."

"I think you should mind your own business."

"You're my brother. You are my business."

"Fine. Mind a different business." Sam took a sip of beer and looked away from Michael so the other man wouldn't notice that he'd really struck a chord with Sam. "Don't you have a fiancée you could be bugging?"

"Alice is nuts about me," Michael said with a grin that slowly faded. "So tell me about you."

"Nothing to tell," Sam lied easily. He wasn't going to dump everything on Michael. There was no reason for it. He'd made his decision and like his father, once his mind was made up, there was no shaking him from it.

"Right." Michael looked around the room. "Hey. When did you paint in here?"

"When I first got here," Sam said. He'd hired a crew to come in and redo his father's office. Hell, he'd been meaning to do it for years but he'd never made the time. But during this trip, the dark maroon walls with their white crown molding had felt as if they were closing in on him.

His father had insisted on dark colors because he claimed they made him calm. Well, Sam didn't remember a time when his father was calm. Or relaxed. And maybe this place had fed into that.

But whether it had or not, Sam hated the darkness of the place, so he'd paid a premium to get a crew in and completely redo not only this damn office, but the whole blasted house. Now the walls were cream colored with pale blue molding and Sam had felt years of depression slide off his shoulders with every room completed.

"It looks better," Michael said. "Wish you looked better, too. But damn Sam…"

"Thanks." Sam sat down and kicked his legs out straight ahead of him. "Maybe I just need a fresh coat of paint."

"We both know what you need, Sam."

He sighed, stared down at the open neck of his beer bottle. "I got a call from my lawyer this morning. He says the divorce papers have *definitely* been filed this time. It'll be official in a couple of months."

"Good news, is it?"

Sam shot him a hard look. "Of course it is. Mia wants a family. Kids. I can't do that."

"Can't or won't?"

"There's no difference."

"Sure there is." Michael took a sip of his beer. "You choose to say no to something—someone— you want. That's won't. Not can't."

"I offered to give her the family she wants. She still said no." Hard to admit. Pain shook him, but he pushed it aside.

"Because she wants you, Sam. She wants you to be there. A part of it all."

"Damn it Michael, I was raised by our father. And you know damn well what a crap role model he was."

"And yet, you're letting *him* decide your life."

"Oh, that's bull." Sam snorted.

"Is it? You're walking away from a woman you love because you think you'll be like Dad."

"Won't I be?" Sam jumped up from the chair because he suddenly couldn't sit still. He walked out onto the stone patio at the rear of the house and looked out over the exquisitely trimmed lawn, the gardens and the ocean beyond.

It was paradise here and yet, for all he noticed, he might as well have been living in someone's garage with a view of a brick wall.

"I can give you one example right now of how

you're not like Dad." Michael walked up beside him, sipped at his beer and stared out over the yard.

When his brother didn't continue, curiosity got the better of Sam. "What?"

"You married Mia. Did Dad ever once marry for love?"

"Well, there's our mother…" Though he'd never seen evidence of love in that relationship.

Michael snorted and as if reading Sam's mind, asked, "Did their marriage look like love to you?" He shook his head. "When I got engaged to Alice, Mom told me how happy she was. She said when they got divorced, Dad told her the only reason he'd married her was *his* father had ordered him to marry her and have at least two children. He wanted to assure the whole Buchanan legacy thing."

That hit Sam harder than it should have. He felt an instant stab of sympathy for his mother that made him even more glad that she'd finally found real love in Sam and Michael's stepfather.

"Yeah, Dad was a prince," Michael muttered. "But my point was, you married Mia because you loved her."

"It still ended."

"Because you let it."

Sam glared at him. "There was nothing I could do. She wanted the divorce, Michael."

"Because you weren't there for her." Michael took a step and stood in front of his brother, forcing Sam to meet his gaze. "I think you were so worried about screwing it up, you stayed away as much as you could. Which was stupid."

"Thanks." He had another sip, but even the beer tasted flat, flavorless. Like the rest of his life.

"No problem. But the solution here is to see what you did wrong and change it."

"She wants kids."

"You do, too," Michael said on a laugh. "You're just scared of screwing that up—and news flash, so's everyone else. So you work at it. You love your kid and you do your best. And I know you, Sam. When you do your best, you never fail."

Was he right? About all of it? Though Michael had been raised by their mother, he'd spent enough time with their dad to know what he was talking about.

Most of his life, Sam had been trying to avoid turning into his father. Yet he'd never noticed that he was nothing like the old man. Just this house was proof of that. The darkness that Sam's father had surrounded himself with had been banished for good. So couldn't he banish darkness from his life, too?

Thinking about Mia again, Sam saw her face in his mind, felt that hard jolt of his heartbeat and knew that whatever else he did in his life would never come close to being as important as his next move would be.

"She filed the papers, Mike," he muttered.

"You've got at least two months before it's final."

Was he right? Should Sam take a good hard look at who he really was? Was it too late?

He looked at his brother. "You gave me a lot to think about, Michael. Thanks."

Michael slapped him on the shoulder. "Any time. Oh. Did I mention that Mia's coming to my wedding?"

Sam looked at him as a slow smile curved his mouth. Suddenly, his breath came a little easier and the day looked a little brighter. "Is that right?"

Mia had to go to Michael's wedding.

She'd always liked Sam's brother and his fiancée was just as nice as he was. Besides, just because she and Sam were finished didn't mean she would give up her relationship with Sam's brother.

But seeing Sam. Being in the same small church with him. Was so much harder than she'd prepared herself for.

The papers had been filed. The divorce would be final in a couple of short months and yet, love still flavored every breath she drew. She'd lived through Christmas with her family and managed to keep her pain from shadowing everyone else's good time.

But she'd gone home from the cruise once again inflating that hope balloon. This time hoping that she might be pregnant. But when that dream died, she had to accept that it was time she let go. Get ready for her appointment at the end of the month. Prepare to welcome her own child and start building the family she wanted so badly.

Sam wouldn't be a part of it and that would always hurt. But she would smile anyway and live the life she wanted.

During the ceremony, she tried to focus on the bride and groom, but her gaze kept straying as if on its own accord, to Sam. So tall, so handsome in his tailored tuxedo. He stood beside his brother and she wondered if he thought about *their* wedding, a little over a year ago. Mia did and the memories brought a pain so bright and sharp it was hard to breathe.

Of course, the two weddings couldn't have been more different. She and Sam had been married on a cliff in Laguna Beach during a bright December morning. Michael and Alice were having a black-tie, evening ceremony in a tiny church that was draped in flowers of white and yellow.

She slipped out of the church from the back row before the bride and groom had a chance to rush smiling down the aisle. She had to try at least to avoid Sam. Otherwise, she'd be a masochist.

Mia hurried out to one of the cars provided by the couple to transport everyone to the reception. The party was being held on one of the Buchanan ships and when she arrived, she saw balloons, streamers, flowers and yellow-and-white garland wrapped along the gangway.

Once aboard, waiters with silver trays holding flutes of champagne greeted the guests. Mia took one and immediately had a long sip. She was going to need it if she was to face Sam.

Flowers lined the route to the main reception,

where a band was playing and every table was decorated with more flowers and candles in hurricane globes that sparkled and shone in the twilight.

She sipped her champagne and avoided the growing crowd in the room by stepping out onto the deck. Here in Florida, the weather was warm, even on a January evening, but the ocean breeze sighed past her in a cool embrace.

"This is good," she whispered to herself. "I'll have to see Sam, but maybe that will help me get over him." It didn't make sense even to her, but Mia hoped it was true.

"Don't get over me."

She took a deep, quick breath and steadied herself by laying one hand on the railing in front of her. Sam. Right there. Behind her.

"Mia—"

"God, Sam," she said, not turning to look at him. "Don't do this to me. Please. Just let me enjoy Michael and Alice's wedding and go home again."

"I can't do that," Sam said softly, then laid his hands on her shoulders and slowly turned her until she was facing him.

He was so handsome he took her breath away. And he wasn't hers. Even the heat slipping into her body from his hands at her shoulders was only temporary. Not hers to keep.

"I'm sorry," he said and simply stunned Mia speechless.

She took a sip of champagne and let the icy bubbles wipe away her suddenly dry throat.

"You're sorry? For what?"

He released her, swept both hands through his hair and then shrugged. "For everything, Mia. I'm sorry I didn't show up for our marriage. Sorry I made you feel as if you weren't important to me when the truth is, you're the *most* important person in my life."

Cautiously, Mia watched him, tried to read his eyes, but too many emotions were dazzling them for her to identify them all. So she waited. To see where he was going with this.

He laughed shortly. "Before I say everything I need you to know, I have to tell you that you're so beautiful, it makes my chest tight."

She laughed too. Mia wasn't a fool. She knew she looked good. She'd made a point of it, since she'd known she'd be seeing Sam. She had wanted him to see her and to be filled with regret for letting her go.

She'd bought a dark red, off-the-shoulder dress with a sweetheart neckline, a cinched waist and a short skirt that stopped mid-thigh. Her black, three-inch heels brought her nearly eye to eye with him, so she could see that he meant what he was saying.

"Thanks. I bought this dress on purpose. To make you suffer."

He laughed again and some of the shadows left his eyes. "Well, mission accomplished."

"What is it you want, Sam?" she asked, bringing them back to the reason he was standing there in front of her.

"You, Mia. I want *you*."

Her heart clutched. "Sam…we've been over this."

"No, no we haven't. Not like we're about to."

She bit her lip and took a breath. "What's that mean?"

"It means," he said, with a rueful shake of his head, "that I finally understand that I'm not just my father's son, but my mother's as well. Mom got past her time with my father. She found love with her second husband and I saw it. They were happy. Hell, Michael grew up in Disneyland comparatively speaking."

"I know your dad was hard, Sam, and I'm sorry about it."

"This isn't about him anymore, Mia." He cupped her face with his hands and stroked his thumbs over her cheekbones. "I've let him go. At last. I finally get that it's my choices that will define my life. Not who my father was."

She stared up into his eyes and read only love shining back at her. Her heart started racing again and that silly balloon of hope was back.

"I want to believe, Sam. I really do."

But how could she? He'd chosen his work over her so many times, she didn't know if he even *could* change.

"Do it, Mia. Believe me. Take one more chance on me. I won't let you down this time. I'm tired of emptiness, Mia. I want the magic and the magic lives inside you. I want real Christmases. I want laughter. Joy. Passion. And that's all with you." His cell phone rang and grumbling, he took it out of his pocket and never checked the screen before he wound up and pitched it over the rail and into the ocean.

"What?" Shocked, she turned to look at the sea then back to him. "What did you just do? That could have been work calling."

"I hope it was," he said firmly and held her again, looking into her eyes, willing her to believe him. "I hate that you're surprised by me choosing you over a business call. You shouldn't have to be. You should have been able to expect that your husband—because we *are* still married—would choose you over business or anything else.

"I'm so sorry for that, Mia. Sorry for not realizing what I had while I had it."

"Oh Sam." Her heart was full and her hands were shaking so badly, champagne sloshed out of her glass onto her hand.

Sam took it and tossed it, too.

"Stop doing that!" Shaking her head, she said, "I never expected you to ignore your work. I love my job at the bakery. I only ever wanted to know that I was important to you, too."

Sam threaded his fingers into her hair and let his gaze move over her face. "You are more important than anything else in my life."

It was so hard to breathe with her heart pounding and the hope balloon swelling until it filled her chest.

"What does that mean for us, Sam?"

"It means I want to stay married. We can have the lawyers pull the divorce papers before they go through."

"Sam…"

"Stay with me, Mia." He kissed her fast. "Make babies with me."

"Really?" She blinked up at him and her eyes filled with tears. She had to blink faster just to clear them.

"I want a family with you. Maybe I always did but I was too scared to even consider it." He bent down and kissed her again, harder, faster. "But I'm more scared of losing you than I am of trying to be a good father."

"You will be a good one," she said. "A great one."

He gave her a half-smile. "I can promise to do my absolute best. I love you, Mia. I will love our kids and we'll have as many as you want. A family with you—a future with you—is all I really want. Mia, you're all I can see of the future. Without you, I don't have one."

"Sam, you're making me cry."

"That's a good sign," he said with a grin. "I like it."

"Of course you do," she said on a laugh.

The first stars appeared overhead and the sounds of the party drifted to them as they stood alone on the deck.

"We'll buy a house anywhere you want," he said quickly as if trying to convince her before her tears dried. "Hell, we can live next door to Maya and Joe."

Now she laughed harder. "Next door might be a little *too* close."

"Okay. That's fine, too. Anything, Mia. Anything to make you happy. I swear I'm a different man."

"Not too different I hope. I always liked—loved— who you were, Sam. I just wanted more of you."

"You'll have it," he swore. "And if I ever do screw up again, you have to call me on it and I'll fix it. I never want to lose you again."

Smiling through her tears, Mia said, "I can't lose you again either, Sam."

"You won't. I swear it." He let her go long enough to dip into his pocket and come out with a ring. He took her right hand in his and slipped the emerald-and-diamond band onto her finger.

When he looked into her eyes this time, he said, "We're already married, so I expect you to put your rings back on when we get home."

She laughed and nodded, looking from the ring to his eyes.

"But this one," he said softly, "I want you to have to mark my promise to you.

"I will love you forever, Mia Harper Buchanan. And I will love the children we make together and I will give you all everything I have."

Mia looked down at the glittering ring on her finger, then up into the most beautiful blue eyes she'd ever seen. "I love you, Sam. Always have. Always will. And I'm so glad you came home."

"You're my home, Mia. My home. My heart. My everything."

And when he kissed her, Mia felt her whole world come right again and she knew that the future stretching out in front of them was filled with all the love she'd ever dreamed of.

* * * * *

Look for these other holiday romances from
USA Today *bestselling author Maureen Child:*

Maid Under the Mistletoe
Tempting the Texan

WE HOPE YOU ENJOYED
THIS BOOK FROM

◆ HARLEQUIN
DESIRE

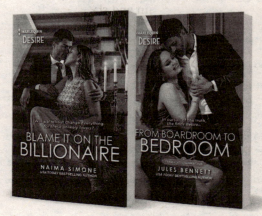

*Luxury, scandal, desire—welcome to
the lives of the American elite.*

Be transported to the worlds of oil barons, family dynasties,
moguls and celebrities. Get ready for juicy plot twists,
delicious sensuality and intriguing scandal.

6 NEW BOOKS AVAILABLE EVERY MONTH!

SPECIAL EXCERPT FROM

Ⓗ HARLEQUIN
DESIRE

*It's Christmas and rancher Creed Cooper must work
with his rival, Wren Maxfield—and tempers flare! But
animosity becomes passion and, now, Wren is pregnant.
Creed wants a marriage in name only. But as desire
takes over, this may be a vow neither can keep…*

Read on for a sneak peek at
Claiming the Rancher's Heir
by New York Times *bestselling author Maisey Yates!*

"Come here," he said, his voice suddenly hard. "I want to show
you something."

There was a big white tent that was still closed, reserved for
an evening hors d'oeuvre session for people who had bought
premium tickets, and he compelled her inside. It was already set
up with tables and tablecloths, everything elegant and dainty,
and exceedingly Maxfield. Though there were bottles of Cowboy
Wines on each table, along with bottles of Maxfield select.

But they were not apparently here to look at the wine, or indeed
anything else that was set up. Which she discovered when he
cupped her chin with firm fingers and looked directly into her eyes.

"I've done nothing but think about you for two weeks. I want
you. Not just something hot and quick against a wall. I need you
in a bed, Wren. We need some time to explore this. To explore
each other."

She blinked. She had not expected that.

He'd been avoiding her and she'd been so sure it was because
he didn't want this.

But he was here in a suit.

And he had a look of intent gleaming in those green eyes.

She realized then she'd gotten it all wrong.

"I…I agree."

She also hadn't expected to agree.

"I want you now," she whispered, and before she could stop herself, she was up on her tiptoes and kissing that infuriating mouth.

She wanted to sigh with relief. She had been so angry at him. So angry at the way he had ignored this. Because how dare he? He had never ignored the anger between them. No. He had taken every opportunity to goad and prod her in anger. So why, why had he ignored this?

But he hadn't.

They were devouring each other, and neither of them cared that there were people outside. His large hands palmed her ass, pulling her up against his body so she could feel just how hard he was for her. She arched against him, gasping when the center of her need came into contact with his rampant masculinity.

She didn't understand the feelings she had for this man. Where everything about him that she found so disturbing was also the very thing that drove her into his arms.

Too big. Too rough. Crass. Untamable. He was everything she detested, everything she desired.

All that, and he was distracting her from an event that she had planned. Which was a cardinal sin in her book. And she didn't even care.

He set her away from him suddenly, breaking their kiss. "Not now," he said, his voice rough. "Tonight. All night. You. In my bed."

Don't miss what happens next in…
Claiming the Rancher's Heir
by New York Times *bestselling author Maisey Yates!*

Available November 2020 wherever
Harlequin Desire books and ebooks are sold.

Harlequin.com

HDEXP1020

Love Harlequin romance?

DISCOVER.

Be the first to find out about promotions, news and exclusive content!

f Facebook.com/HarlequinBooks

🐦 Twitter.com/HarlequinBooks

📷 Instagram.com/HarlequinBooks

📌 Pinterest.com/HarlequinBooks

ReaderService.com

EXPLORE.

Sign up for the Harlequin e-newsletter and download a free book from any series at **TryHarlequin.com**

CONNECT.

Join our Harlequin community to share your thoughts and connect with other romance readers! **Facebook.com/groups/HarlequinConnection**

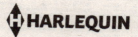

HARLEQUIN

HSOCIAL2020